FROM THE PORCH

SHORT STORIES

FROM THE PORCH

SHORT STORIES

Majel Stites Redick

for Roger

ACKNOWLEDGMENTS

The author wishes to acknowledge those individuals who have given love, support, editing assistance, encouragement, and a listening ear:
Phyllis Scott
Doug Rainbow
Shirley Moore
Fred Tarpley, Professor Emeritus of
Literature and Languages
TAMU – Commerce, TX

Many thanks.

CONTENTS

I.

ABOUT STEWART

1

ROBERTA

It happened at the Stockyards in Ft. Worth. He was a bachelor who trained, bought, and sold horses. Ken was a tall handsome young man of medium build with deep blue eyes. All the girls paid attention to him astride a horse.

She was a petite brown-eyed brunette with a knockout figure. She wore men's Levis, a sleeveless white blouse and beautifully tooled cowboy boots. Roberta and her girlfriend had come to the Stockyards Rodeo to meet guys. They weren't much interested in the horses, just the riders and owners.

Roberta and Ken had a whirlwind courtship (well let's say one-night stand), got married, and he took her home to his little horse ranch in East Texas. She had been glad to return the borrowed cowboy boots. Didn't fit her anyway. What difference did it make?

She'd found a man. Roberta really didn't care about big, smelly horses and manure and sweat. *I can change all that later*, she decided.

* * *

Roberta was six years younger than Ken, but she had been so cute and bubbly. After they married and she got settled in, he learned she really had no love for ranch life at all. Ken kept the place up and the business grew. Roberta found new interests and wants.

"But Ken, you don't even have to use a wringer. The washing machine is electric and does it all for you. It has it's own, its own... agitator!"

Ken laughed, bought the new washer and the dryer. She was excited. He showed her how to load the clothes.

"See, you put them in like this. No not that. My old dirty jeans don't' go in there with your clothes and Stewie's tee shirts. Then you push this button and it will fill up with hot water. No, not that one, this one."

"Oh Kenny! Thank you!" She threw her arms around his neck, gave him a great big kiss and went and sat down in front of the television.

He gave her other bright, shiny appliances she pleaded for. The Mixmaster made her eyes sparkle so.

"Oh wow! I can make Stewie a birthday cake!" The mixer sat on the countertop unused.

He gave in again on the furniture. She thought it needed updating. He moved his old favorite couch out to the screened in porch. He let her buy the car she wanted, another bright shiny appliance. She made good use of it though. Roberta ran around with girlfriends, went on shopping trips, visited flea markets, seemed to always have activities away from him and Stewart.

* * *

Today would change Ken's life. Poor unsuspecting man, he didn't know it yet. He finished up with the horses, walked out of the barn into the bright sunlight, and squinted. He leaned on his pitchfork and slapped his gloves against his leg. When he reached into his overalls to stick the gloves in his pocket, he pulled out an old wrinkled bandana, reached up and wiped the sheen of sweat off his forehead. He started slowly toward the house.

The wood frame house sat back about a hundred yards from the old blacktop road, and huge oaks and maples lined its driveway. A screened-in porch extended across the front of the house. The freshly painted barn stood just beside and a little to the north of the house.

When Roberta had given birth to Stewart, she told Ken, "No more kids." She ignored the baby much of the time and seemed to center her life around TV, the endless running around and dishing dirt with her girlfriends. And chain smoking.

Ken made a good income off horses; training them for people, offering stables, grooming, riding lessons, and occasional trail rides. He loved his horses more than anything. Well, almost anything. He was crazy about Stewie and wanted him to grow up knowing horses. Roberta would scream her head off anytime he mentioned taking Stewie up on the Chugger for a ride with him.

The side screen door slammed as Ken walked into the kitchen. He could hear the television. He looked into the living room and saw Roberta watching a game show. She had on an old wrinkled blouse and pajama bottoms. Her bare feet were propped up on the couch, and she was flicking the ashes from her cigarette toward an ashtray on the coffee table.

"Where's Stewie?"

"Sshhh! Curt just asked the Magic Question," She pointed toward the TV with her cigarette. "In his room playing. "

About that time Stewie ran into the room, a big grin on his face, and shouted "Daddy!"

Ken bent to swing him up in the air. "Hey, Stewie, guy. What's goin' on?"

"Hungwy, Daddy."

Ken put him down and patted him on the back. "Go on in the kitchen, son. Daddy'll come get you somethin' to eat."

Roberta squealed as some goofy guy on TV answered the Magic Question correctly.

Ken walked over to the couch. "Roberta, it's after 12:30. Haven't you fed the boy yet?"

"I was just gettin' ready to."

"Well, come on in the kitchen and eat with us. I've got to go to town this afternoon to get some feed; then I have to go to the hardware store, and I thought we'd go by and pick up a few groceries. After we eat, get you and Stewie cleaned up. Don't take long now, we need to get started."

"I don't wanna go."

"What do you mean, don't wanna go? Of course you'll go."

Roberta's voice got whiney. "Oh, Kenny. Don't make me go. I just don't feel like it. You go ahead and take Stewie. Both of you can eat at the Tasty Spoon before you come home."

Ken's voice had a sharp edge to it. "No, Roberta, I will NOT take Stewie. I have too much to get done." He turned and walked into the kitchen. Roberta stubbed out her cigarette, rose, and followed behind him.

Stewie looked up from the table where he sat, ready to eat, and said, "Go, Daddy?"

"No, son. You need to stay here and take care of your momma."

"I may go over to Earline's for a while."

"You mean you're able to get up off your butt for that? I thought you didn't feel good."

"Well, I don't, really, but Earline and I won't do anything except chat and watch TV. Then she remembered. "And Stewie can play on the floor in front of us."

Ken looked at her, a long hard stare.

"I may stop over by Cliff's to see his new pickup and take a look at that horse he was telling me about. You and Stewie go ahead and eat without me."

As Ken walked out of the room he said, "Bye, Stewie, take good care of your momma."

As soon as Ken's pickup pulled out of the driveway, Roberta went in and started putting on makeup, the kind of heavy makeup she thought made her look sexy. She changed clothes and put on a bright pink knit top, with a vee neck, and some new red polyester slacks, just a wee bit too tight. Roberta knew red and pink weren't supposed to go together; but she also knew how eye-catching the duo was. She put on her red plastic slide-in sandals with the two-inch heels. She knew, too, these made her butt look good. She added some big, shiny dangly earrings. She took one last look at herself in the mirror. Oooh. Those bright sparklies looked good. "Girl, you are one hot dish."

She grabbed a washcloth and swiped at Stewie's face. She noticed the tomato soup stains on his tee shirt but grabbed his little arm and half dragged, half jerked him toward the door.

"OW, Momma!"

Roberta tuned the car radio to a country station. All the way to town Stewie tried to talk over the sound of the music.

"Look, Momma," he would point out the window.

"Momma, what's . . .?"

"Hush, baby. Momma's tryin' to think," she said as she changed radio stations and flicked another cigarette butt out the window.

When Roberta and Stewie got to town, she parked in front of the town's only drugstore, went in, and pulled Stewie along the aisle until she got to the back where the hair dye was.

She picked up box after box and looked at the hair colors of the women on the front. All the while Stewie chattered. She paid no attention to him, but he stuck right by her side.

Roberta read the back of one box, with a pretty blonde pictured on the front, and said "Baby, your momma's gonna be a blonde." She took the box up front to the checkout counter.

Stewie looked up at her and grinned, "Bwonde?"

The clerk eyed Roberta, picked the box up off the counter and looked at it. Roberta noticed he had a pitted face and horn-rimmed glasses, but he was built pretty well.

"Well hello little guy" he grinned down at Stewie. "Your Momma going to get even prettier than she already is?"

"Momma pwetty."

Roberta smiled her big flirty smile at the clerk, paid, and walked out the door. "Like a Million Dollars," she said to herself.

Down the street was a lighted beer sign over the tavern. She walked in, headed up to the bar and said, "I'll have a beer." She noticed out of the corner of her vision that every eye in the place was on her.

"Lady, you can't bring that child in here."

She had forgotten Stewie, who looked up and said "Momma beer?"

"Oh, that's just Stewie. He won't bother anything." She gave the bartender that smile.

"Doesn't make any difference, Ma'am. It's against the law."

Roberta used her *I'll be darned* voice. "You mean a lady can't come in here and have a nice cold beer? It's re-a-l-ly warm out there."

"It's against the law with the kid, Ma'am."

"Well," she knew she had captured the attention of the other customers, "do you suppose that lady could get a cold six–pack to take home and drink all by her lonesome?"

He reached down and brought up a cardboard carton of six bottles and scooted it across the bar.

She batted her eyes and said, "And maybe a bag to put it in?"

He came up with a paper bag. Then she paid and tugged Stewie out the door, feeling all the while the attention her figure was drawing.

Roberta knew that Ken didn't want any alcohol in the house. But this was the day she had decided to declare "A New You," like the advertisement on TV talked about.

When she and Stewie got home, Roberta made him sit down in front of the television while she went to dye her hair. It took a long time. First she had to wash and put rollers in it, then apply the bleach. She took drinks of beer in between each step of the process.

She kept checking to see if the boy was still in front of the TV. He was. The dye burned a little bit at first, but then settled down to a sting.

She opened another beer and giggled while she was waiting for her hair to bleach, giggled and decided pain was the price of beauty.

Stewie got up once and came into the bathroom and looked up at her. "Takin' care of Momma?"

"Yes, baby. Momma's gonna be a blonde. You'll love your Momma's blonde hair."

"Momma bwonde." He want back and sat in front of the TV.

It was getting late in the afternoon by the time she finished and uncovered her hair. When she saw it, how white it was, she just *knew* Ken would make her wear a scarf to church. It was actually platinum, and she was really excited about it.

She dried it and started unrolling it. Little tufts of hair came out. She couldn't believe it! She patted and rubbed, and started crying. The more she cried the worse it got.

When she ran the comb through it, handfuls came out. "A-a-a-h-h-h E-**E-E-H**!" she screamed at the top of her lungs, until she ran out of breath.

Stewie came running in.

"Momma! Momma!"

"Stewart," she gasped out, "**go sit** on the **porch**. And don't you get UP til I come and get you."

"Momma bwonde?" He went to the porch.

Roberta opened another beer, blew her nose, and avoided touching her head. It was on fire now.

She went out on the porch with her beer and sat down on the couch beside Stewie. She was gulping beer, her head was on fire, and she was sobbing.

Stewie sat there quietly with tears running down his face. "Momma?"

Roberta sucked in her breath. "Momma loves you baby. You just sit right here. Don't you MOVE til your Daddy gets home."

"Wuv you, Momma." He obeyed.

She went in, tied a scarf around her throbbing head, re-applied her make up, and packed her suitcase.

When she walked out the front door, balancing a beer in one hand, suitcase in the other, she said, "Now, remember, Stewart. Sit there til your Daddy gets here."

Stewie was still sniffling, his eyelids growing heavy. "Momma bwonde. Takin care . . ."

Roberta got in the car and drove off.

Stewie was curled up in a little ball sleeping when Ken got home.

They never saw Roberta again.

2

KEN AND STEWART

When Ken Wilkes' wife left him, he had a son to raise alone. He looked after his property, his horses, and the framework of their lives. He and Stewart made a life for one another. When Stew was still young, Ken tried to get a babysitter to come in and help occasionally. He was busy all the time with his horse business. He had to leave the place for sales or to get equipment repaired, to do his banking business. He needed care for Stewie. He tried using high school kids, but all they did was sit in front of the TV with Stew and snack. Just like having Roberta back.

Different women from around the community had come by and offered. Nyla Vernon from the church made two or three overtures.

"Ken, you need a woman to take care of you and Stew." Or "Wouldn't you like to have a mother figure around to help you raise the boy?"

Nyla was a very attractive brunette with a nice figure and a pleasant way about her. Ken had ideas about having her around, but they didn't involve any full-time commitment. He hesitated to be frank about it because he certainly didn't want any church gossip. He breathed a sigh of relief when she married a man from Little Rock and moved away. The entire First Baptist Church of Yancey Crossing was invited. Ken and Stewie didn't go to the wedding.

There were others, but they all seemed pushy and desperate. Ken didn't really go out looking. Sure he had yearnings, but the right one never came along. Finally it just worked out easier for him to take Stewie wherever he went.

He was a good kid, and Ken decided he was learning about family, and people, and life just fine.

They shopped for groceries.

"Daddy, I like the snappy cereal that crackles in my ear!"

They cooked together.

"Pop, I can stir the gravy."

"Be careful not to burn yourself."

So they shopped and cooked and ate meals together. They attended horse shows as a team, and worked side by side at the ranch. Ken and little Stewart did everything as one.

When Stewie was big enough, Ken gave him chores to do around the place, making him keep his room and himself clean and neat. Got him to help sweep out the stalls. He sent him off to school every day, paid attention to Stew's homework, and acted like he thought a good daddy should act. He showed him how to scrub the back of his neck and behind his ears; showed him how to lay out the clothes he would wear to school, and later to cook entire meals.

Ken read to his son every night; tried to make it something different each time, though Stewie would ask for the one about *"This is milady, this is me lad"* over and over.

* * *

Ken continued to take Stewie to Sunday School and church. From the time he was very young, Ken had Stew listen to him read a Bible passage every day. After Stew learned to read, Ken had him read a Bible verse out loud every night after supper. He was very patient about Stew's hesitations and pronunciations, and he always lent a hand or an encouraging word.

The day, and the question, finally came.

"Pop, what happened to my momma?"

After long, hard thought Ken replied. "Son, she went away. We didn't know she was going. We don't know where she went, but I think she just didn't like living here."

Silence.

"I know you didn't do anything to make her go away. And I know she loved you very much."

"Then why doesn't she come and see me, Pop?"

Ken felt as if his heart was tearing in two.

"Well, Stew, I think she just got busy." He waited for the next question, but it never came.

"Okay, Pop. Good night."

* * *

More than once Ken wished he could just get up and walk away. *Lord, I know I need help bringing up my son, please guide me. Help me find what it takes to raise this boy right.* Sometimes he thought getting married was the right answer, but God never led him in that direction.

* * *

For a time in his evening scripture reading, Stewie would just open the Bible, put his finger on a verse, and read it to his dad. After a while, Ken would assign things for Stew to read, and to do this he would ask specific questions: "Tell me who Moses was." "What did Jesus say about that?" "What happened to Peter?" "Who wrote this Psalm?" Again, he tried to be very patient while Stew did his homework and his Bible history.

* * *

At times Ken's responsibilities really weighed him down.

I want to run out there, jump in my pickup, go drink a few beers. Find a woman and some softness in life. Oh Lord. Help me. Guide me.

Stew learned a great deal about the Bible early on. As he grew older, Ken made him pick verses every week and memorize them. One day after school Stew ran in, they ate supper, and then it was time for him to recite his Bible verse.

"John 11:35. Jesus Wept." He turned and started for the door.

"Hey! What do you think you're getting by with?" Ken asked.

"Sorry, Dad. Annette Gibson invited me over to study with her tonight. Don't have much time."

Stew was fifteen now. Against Ken's better judgment he asked, "You want to borrow the pickup?"

"No, thanks. I'll saddle up Chugger. Maybe we'll go horseback riding after we study."

As Stew got his books to go, Ken said, "A little moonlight ride, huh?" to the slamming screen door.

* * *

Stew worked hard, studied hard and was a good, responsible kid. Ken figured pretty soon Stew would be sixteen and graduating.

When Stew graduated high school, Ken bought a used car from one of his horse tradin' friends.

"Well, Stew, I figure you're on your way to college and to being on your own. You need a car."

"Wow Pop! I never thought about having to do without the Chugger. Thanks a lot." His face lit up, but there was a catch in his voice.

* * *

Stew went to college at Oklahoma State on a scholarship from the Equine Foundation. He packed up a few clothes, some old horse magazines, toiletries, and a faded picture of a young Ken on a young Chugger with a pretty brunette standing looking up at them.

He spent time in classes, time in the library studying, and at his part-time job cleaning in the Department of Animal Husbandry horse barns. He also spent his share of time in front of his roommate's TV staring at Twilight Zone episodes; but it was all just marking time for him. He didn't know what he was waiting for.

Close to the end of the second semester Ken got a phone call from Stew late one Saturday evening.

"Hiya Pop. Whatcha' doin'? "

"Listening to the baseball game on the radio. I figured you'd be out on a date on a Saturday night."

"Naw. . .

"What's wrong, son?"

"Oh nothin' much."

Pause.

"Stewart, have you been kicked out of school?"

"Aw dammit, Pop. I wrecked my car."

"Are you okay? Was anybody hurt?"

"I'm okay. Nobody's hurt."

In a very severe voice, "Stewart Wilkes, don't you ever let me hear you curse like that again. As far as the accident, I'm glad you're safe and nobody was hurt. As far as the car goes, you have insurance to deal with, and the rest of that business. You have to decide what you're going to do. You've always been a responsible boy. Now it's time for you to take on a man's responsibilities. I don't need to know what was involved, whether girls, drinking, carelessness or whatever. I just need

24

to know that you use your good sense to get it handled."

"Okay, Pop. I know I screwed up, and you can trust me to take care of it."

"Stewart, how are your classes going?"

"Good, Pop. Still all A's except for the History. Barely maintaining my C."

Ken could hear an Elvis song playing in the background. "Son, I love you. Take care."

"Bye, Daddy. I love you."

* * *

Stew went to the university for two years. Ken didn't know exactly what went on, but after two years, three girlfriends, and one wrecked car, Stew withdrew from school and joined the Marines. Ken was bewildered by this decision but tried not to show it and to give Stew his moral support. He figured he'd taught Stew the basics, and the boy/man had been making his own decisions for quite a while.

Stew was sent straight to Viet Nam and was gone four years. He kept in touch with Ken, but he was occupied with fighting a war. The letters were few and far between. Sometimes Ken was so tired it was easier to ride Chugger out to the mailbox than to walk; but he did what a lot of parents were doing. He prayed and put a letter in the mail every Monday.

.

3

REENA

Reena had been married to Bud Loyd almost thirty-five years the day he dropped over dead painting the mailbox. She married Bud when she was sixteen years old. Moved right off her Daddy's Oklahoma farm to Bud's farm twelve miles south. She started raising chickens and sons, with a few dogs and cats and rabbits thrown in here and there over the years.

When Bud died her two sons came home and helped her settle all they could. Bud Jr. was a career Marine stationed in Guam. Tommy was married, living in California. She thought Tommy and his wife had both acted, well, strange. She couldn't quite put her finger on it. After things were settled, both boys went on back to their lives.

* * *

Reena felt at odds without Bud. No one to cook for, or clean up after, or argue with. She couldn't bear sitting on the front porch by herself.

Finally, Reena sold the farm and bought Widow Richard's little house on the north edge of town. Then she became Widow Lloyd. She planted flowers. She planted tomato plants. She planted cucumbers. She didn't get much of a crop. She visited all her neighbors and looked over their gardens. She finally drove over to Yancey Crossing, bought tomatoes, and canned 12 quarts before she ran out of jars.

The Widow Richards' son, who sold Reena the house, came over calling. Hack Richards talked with her just like they'd known one another all their lives. She liked hearing the tales about his job. He took her to the swapmeet in Cooleyville.

"Come on, Miz Reena, let me buy you that bracelet. It'll look real pretty on you.

"Don't wear jewelry."

"Well, then how about we stop some-where on the way home and I buy you a cold soda pop?" She laughed and agreed.

Reena remembered sitting out on the front porch with Bud every night after supper. The quiet times.

Hack came calling again. Drove her all the way to Yancey Crossing to have dinner at the Tasty Spoon. It was a nice spread.

"Did you ever make chicken and dumplins?"

"Oh my yes." Reena said. "One of the boys was always glad to go kill me a big fat hen 'cause they knew what was comin'."

"My mama used to make the best fried chicken. I always got the livers and gizzards."

The talk was easy and Reena noticed what a huge amount of food Hack ate. She liked a man who ate hearty, but this was ridiculous.

"I declare I never saw anyone put away that much food."

"Yeah, always been a good eater."

Good Lord, he thinks that's a compliment.

Hack Richards kept coming around. He fixed her front gate. Dug a compost pit in the garden for her. One night he took her to the Hole in the Wall. They drank a few beers and listened to the jukebox. Hack knew everybody in town, and they all chatted, laughed, and stopped by the booth to say Hi to Hack and meet Reena. It was a real friendly group.

Next morning Reena had a bad headache, but she couldn't remember when she had laughed so hard. Couldn't remember what had been so funny, either.

Reena married Hack Richards at the county courthouse the following Thursday. Then she called her sons and told them they had a new stepdaddy. Neither of them seemed surprised or interested.

Buddy Jr. said, "I hope he's good to you, Mama."

Tommy said, "Well, congratulations, I guess."

* * *

"What does that bunch look like to you?" Bud would say, pointing at the night sky.

"I see a big long sweep, like the wind is blowin' all the stars across heaven.

"What do you see?"

"It looks like your face the day we found out you were expecting."

"Oh, Bud Loyd. Don't never!" She imitated swatting him. Soft chuckling from the porch.

* * *

Hack Richards traveled around the Southwest selling fishing lures to variety stores. He also traveled around to a variety of bars. Most nights when he was home he sat in front of the TV and drank beer till he passed out snoring. Some of the time he was at the Hole in the Wall drinking until closing time.

Reena missed Bud.

"Where's Tommy?"

"He rode with the kids in the bus to the football game over in Collinsville."

She could remember the sound of both rockers creaking against the boards of the porch in the stillness of the night.

Once Hack went on a fishing trip with two guys from the bar. Three days later Reena got a call from a man in Ralston. The guys had wrecked Hack's van and gotten thrown out of two bars in Collinsville. Then two of them hitched a ride to Ralston and passed out in the local bar there. The Ralston bartender found Reena's phone number in Hack's billfold, and called her to come get them.

As she drove, her mind drifted back.

"Where did Buddy go?"

"He went to Wilkes' house. Stew's helping him with this algebra."

"Whoo-eee. They can have that algebra." Soft *twilight laughter.*

* * *

Before she knew it, Reena was in Ralston. She walked into the bar, straining and puffing. She was scooting a giant red Coleman cooler. She dragged it across the floor to Hack's feet. He had his head down on the table and didn't stir. She walked up to the bar and said, "These jerks owe you any money?"

"No ma'am. Just get'em outta here and we'll call it even."

"Mister, you and me don't have nothin to git even about." She opened her big lime green purse and slapped three dollars on the bar. "Gimme a beer, change for that payphone over there and about fifteen minutes. I'll have 'em cleared outta here" motioning to the two drunks passed out at the table.

Reena walked over to the payphone, lifted the receiver, and dialed.

"Hello, Billy? Reena Lloyd. Yeah, Richards. Oh, about three months now. That's part of what I wanna talk to you about. How's Lillian? Oh, bless her heart. I canned my last ones in July. I got twelve quarts settin' on the shelf. That's my last cannin'."

The bar was quiet except for an occasional snort or gasp from the fishermen. Hack raised his head up off the table, belched, and said "Izzat you Reena honey?" He looked around blankly then flopped his head back down on his arms.

The bartender tried to act busy, but other customers made no pretense of doing anything except listening to Reena's side of the phone conversation.

Reena had dragged a barstool over by the payphone, climbed up on it, and was just as relaxed as if she was in her own kitchen.

"Well, Billy. What I called about is Hack Richards. Yes. I'm over here at Ralston at . . . hell, I don't even know the name of this place."

About five voices chorused "Town Talk."

"Yeah. The Town Talk tavern. Hack and one of his buddies is passed out drunk. They wrecked Hack's car. No, no. I don't suppose so. I do suspect they been fishin' without a license, though. Now listen, Billy. Why don't you just send one of your deputies over here to pick'em up and let'em sleep it off down at county jail for a couple of days?"   A long pause as Reena listened.

"Thanks, Billy. Appreciate it."

Old Fisherman number two, raised his head up from the table and said in a loud voice, "Bring us two more" before his head plopped back on the table.

Reena continued with her phone conversation. Her voice became very slow and distinct. "One other thing. There's a big red cooler that goes with Hack. Oh, no. Not that. It's his clothes. It's his shavin' kit. A picture of his momma in a little silver frame. A little paper bag full of lures and a carton of Camels.

Billy, when you let him out of jail, this cooler goes with him. Yeah, Billy, but it don't come back to my house. You got that? It don't dome back to my house or my street. Or next time he goes fishin it won't just be without a license, it'll be without his worm. Got that, Billy? Where I come from people get shot for less than that. Yes. Thanks a lot. You and Lillian come by sometime, you hear? Bye, Bye."

When Reena hung up the phone, there was a little coughing and shuffling around, and the bar patrons turned their attention back to their beer. Reena got up, moved the bar stool back to the bar and scooped up her change. She never touched the beer.

"You don't have to worry" she told the bartender. "The county sheriff's boys will be here in a little bit and clean them two outta here for ya."

With that she adjusted the strap of her big green purse on her shoulder, walked out the door, and drove straight to the county courthouse where she got Neal, one of Tommy's high school classmates, to draw up divorce papers.

4

STEWART AND REENA

Reena had worked all her life and wasn't ready to stop yet. At fifty-two she had thirty-five good years with Bud;, three mistaken months with Hack Richards, and now the chance to do something on her own.

When she looked into the mirror, it was just to run a comb through her unruly hair, reddish going gray. A bystander would see a short woman with a sturdy figure, weathered face, and a wide, ready smile. When she laughed, it came out as a deep, throaty chuckle.

Reena knew she had a strong back and plenty of energy. She just didn't know what to do with it. On Monday morning she went down to the nursing center, talked to Nadine Simms, and filled out an application for nurse's aide. She started work on Thursday. She was rough talking, and sometimes the staff cringed at the way Reena let fly with her words and her emotions. They noticed, too, how good she was with elderly patients, and how gentle she was with her hands

Reena ran into Stewart Wilkes at the nursing center. She'd heard he was home from the war. Stewart had gone to high school with her boys, and had been in the same class as Tommy, her youngest. When her oldest, Bud Jr. signed up after graduation and joined the Marines, he tried to talk Stewart Wilkes into joining up with him.

She could hear Buddy, Jr. now. C'mon Stew, we'll be Viet Nam war buddies, Semper Fi!"
Instead the Wilkes boy had gone to the state university for a while before he joined the Marines and was sent to Viet Nam.

Bud Jr. had made a career out of the military. It was his way of dealing with life. It was his only approach and the only way he could cope, and Reena understood this.

Then there was this Wilkes boy. He was always a good kid, a polite boy. Reena didn't know how old man Wilkes had done it, raised that boy with no momma. Mr. Wilkes and the boy were both quiet, soft-spoken, and people liked them. They had been involved in church stuff a lot, and Reena had wanted her boys to do that, too. But she never pushed church on them because she didn't know how.

* * *

Tommy had gone over to Stew's house some when they were growing up, and he was fascinated by Stew's life with his Dad, the horses, his Bible reading, and all the books.

"Whaddya mean they got books, son? You got books, too."

"Yeah, but Momma, I don't mean like Readers Digest. They got books on the walls. Books with no pictures on the covers. Books with hard backs and stuff. Not just schoolbooks. And I think Stewie reads all them books."

"Tommy, I don't know what to tell you. Except sometime you might ask Stew to tell you about what all's in them books."

* * *

When Stewart came home from Viet Nam, Mr. Wilkes had suffered a stroke and been in the nursing home for about three months. Stewart came to the home every day and spent four or five hours with his daddy. He shaved him.

"Stew son, be more careful with that razor. After all those weapons, seems to me like you could be dangerous to your old dad."

"Don't worry, Pop. If you see me coming with a knife like I'm going to stab you, THEN you can put up a fight."

He combed his dad's hair.

"Remember that first time I took you to Rufus down at the barber shop?"

"Seems kinda like I really wanted up in that big monster chair."

"Oh you wanted up there all right, til about the time Rufus turned on the clippers." Ken and Stew both hee-hawed over that one.

"Oh yeah, I remember. You had to spank my butt to make me sit still. I think it only made me cry harder."

"Yup" Ken said softly.

Stew read aloud to his daddy. He'd bring a sack of blackberries, or a big red ripe tomato or a peach. He'd peel it and slice it and they'd share it. Ken often complained about Stew getting a bigger share.

"Stew, you need more practice with your knife weapon. Seems like you always cut that tomato to you're benefit, not mine."

Stew would speak to Reena, make small talk. He asked about her boys. The two of them would chit chat about her garden, his peach tree. He was always warm and courteous to her.

Reena had heard that Stewart Wilkes spent his evenings at the local tavern drinking and carousing. It seemed out of character to her, he'd always been such a respectable kid. She admired the way he took care of his daddy. And she sure didn't believe in all that wild gossip her co-workers would pass around in the staff lounge. One day in the lunch room, she said, "Where I come from, if you cain't say somethin good about some-body, you don't say nothin at all." That brought few smiles and a halt to the conversa-tion. They all exchanged looks behind her back.

* * *

Stewart read something out of the Bible to his daddy every day. And he'd read a letter to the editor, or a horse journal article, a hunt-ing story out of Field and Stream. *"and listen to this, Pop, he ended up hooking a 32 pound cat-fish."*

Sometimes he would read out of those hardback books. Or paperbacks. One time he started reading a story out loud about an old man in a boat. Reena hung close to the room all she could, and would dally around out in the hall trying to hear the story. The old man was trying to catch a fish. It took days for

Stewart to read that story. Sometimes Mister Wilkes would just close his eyes and lie there and listen. Sometimes he would sleep. Stew would continue reading.

Reena could tell when it was getting close to the end of the story. She quit all pretense of listening from the hallway. She just walked in that day and sat down in the extra chair in Mr. Wilkes' room. Stewart glanced up, winked and nodded his head at Reena, and kept on reading. His voice would get very soft and low and rise and fall just like the waves in the ocean around the old man's boat. Reena was mesmerized by the story and found herself holding her breath.

"Up the road, in his shack, the old man was sleeping again. He was still sleeping on his face and the boy was sitting by him watching him. The old man was dreaming about the lions."

The story ended, and she was about to sob. Instead she sucked some air in between her teeth and let a big tear roll down her cheek and off the end of her nose.

Stew very gently closed the book. Holding the front and back covers between his palms like a prayer, he stood and laid the book on the dresser. He leaned over and patted his daddy's hand. His father clutched at Stewart's fingers, looked up at him, smiled and winked.

Reena felt like an eavesdropper. She rose from the chair, and as she tried to slip out the door, Stewart turned and started toward the window. He reached out and squeezed her shoulder. When she walked out, he was standing with his back to the room, gazing out the window.

5

ANNETTE

During the four years Stew spent in Viet Nam, Ken was aging, breaking down and wearing out, like an old horse. When his health got so bad he couldn't keep the place up, he leased his house and business to a family from Yancey Crossing. They had kids who could help with the horses and learn all the things Stew had grown up around.

When Stew returned home, his Daddy was in a nursing home. Stewart offered to buy out the remainder of the lease on his Daddy's place, and the couple took him up on it. They were ready to get back to city life. They parted amicably, and Stew moved back into his own home place.

He spent much of his days with his Dad, visiting with him, swapping stories about their lives and just hanging out. And reading to him. Evenings on his way home, he would stop in at the Hole-in-the-Wall and have a few drinks. shoot the bull with the guys, flirt with the girls a while, then head home.

Hi, Handsome. Buy a girl a drink?

I don't believe a sweet young thing like you drinks alcohol.

Oh, I don't. I just sip along and listen to the music and watch the dancing. You like to dance?

Stew would get off his bar stool and twirl them around the dance floor a couple of times, but nothing much ever came of it. He'd just smile and think about how he and Ken talked of women.

Stew wasn't physically or emotionally up to minding the horses, so he and his daddy agreed, and he sold them at auction. But he couldn't give up Chappy, his Dad's favorite. Grand old chestnut, Chugger had been Stewart's own childhood favorite, and Chappy was Chugger's offspring.

* * *

When Ken Wilkes died from complications of pneumonia, Stewart handled everything the way his dad had always taught him to, quickly, efficiently, respectfully. Endless, agonizing, meticulous details. The preacher gave a fine service. Stew, with no other living relatives, felt gathered up by the crowd. There were all the neighbors, the entire congregation from Yancey Crossing Baptist, Ken's friends from the horse circuit, and many of Ken's friends from long ago days. Stew knew that everyone loved Ken, but he was humbled by the number of his own friends from his youth and high school who showed up. He was overwhelmed by the loss of Ken.

He went home to try healing his spirit. He'd ride Chappy up the bridle trails, through the woods, and gallop across the back pastures until they were both worn out and sweaty. Neighbors would drop by to bring a covered dish, or stop and visit a while. He got tickled about the young single gals and divorcees who suddenly started calling, or just dropping by to check on him. He and Ken had shared many stories about single women and their subtleties and their nesting instincts.

One young widow and two divorcees had tried to catch his daddy for years. One divorcee, Carrie, had been relentless in her pursuit of Ken. Stewart had hated her, not because she was trying to snare Ken, not because she simpered over the motherless Stew, but because she was the worst cook in Harkin County. Stew had once asked Ken if it was okay to pray for Miss Carrie not to bring them anymore pies or casseroles. His dad had slapped his knee laughing about that.

All this was just funny to Stew until the day Annette called.

"Hello, Stewart. It's Annette." There was a long pause. "You know, Annette Gibson."

"My gosh, Annette. Where are you?"

"Oh, I'm over at the folks place, visiting Mom and Dad."

"No, I mean where do you live now?"

"Oh, I've been in D.C., practicing law there."

"Gee, Annette, it's so great to hear your beautiful voice. I've wondered for a long time where you'd gone."

"Well, that's why I called. The folks just told me about Mr. Wilkes. Stew, your daddy was always so kind to me, such a gentle man. I thought I might drop by to see you."

"Sure, sweetie, I'll be glad to see you any time."

"Is now okay?"

6

INTERLUDE

Stewart had spent his days at the nursing home with his Dad and his evenings dropping by the Hole-in-the-Wall.

After his daddy died, Stew kept up his habit of hanging around the tavern. Days were spent around the home place; going for horseback rides with Annette, her on her dad's big buckskin, Legend, him on Chappy. They'd ride up through the hills. He'd make a thermos of coffee; she'd pack some sandwiches and an apple or a couple of peaches.

As she mounted Legend one day, she said with a quick giggle, "I'll race you to the high meadow, come see what's waiting."

They'd find a sunny knoll, or a shady hollow, lie on a saddle blanket and make love. He'd peel a peach for her with his pocketknife and feed her little slices. They'd eat sandwiches, drink coffee, laugh, swap stories and snuggle in silent embraces listening to the sounds of the trees.

Annette told Ken about her life in D.C. legal circles, her longing to be back home, and her loneliness among the people of the city.

"Oh, Stew, it was all so competitive. I competed for a place in the firm. I competed for the attention of the partners. There was even competition for a place in line at the supermarket counter. And the traffic! It was nightmarish. Drivers in D.C. were all on the offense. It was nerve-racking. I wanted to come home and see if I could start my own little practice. Small town folks with…I don't know. With different values, just regular people."

Stew would tell her secrets about himself, his lack of ambition, and his loneliness for Ken. But he always steered the conversation away from his activity in Viet Nam, refused to talk about his health problems. He knew she noticed but she didn't pry. He wanted to talk about it, but it seemed too personal; even more intimate than the physical union they shared.

Stew told her the about one time when he had come to her house to study. Ken had teased him about going on a moonlight horse-back ride.

"I don't know why I ignored his remark" said Stew.

"Oh, silly. You were going through puberty. You felt guilty or embarrassed that your Dad had such ideas. Or that he could read your mind," she grinned up at him.

"I guess you're right, I never saw Daddy that way. But he was a teenager once, too."

There was a quiet pause.

"Do you ever wonder about your mother?"

Slowly, "No-o-o. Well. I did for a while when I was in grade school. When I started to grow up a little I was jealous of the other kids who had moms. Later I realized Daddy had lived his whole life for me, but . . ." the sentence died into silence.

After an interminable pause, "In 'Nam I had a buddy who encouraged me to search for her." Then, in short terse bursts, "Considered it. Not seriously. Let it drop. Seemed like a futile attempt to hunt for something I didn't want.

Annette laid her head on his shoulder, and he held her. Before she left she said "Moonlight ride tomorrow night?"

"You're on."

Sometimes she'd come over in the evenings and they'd cook dinner together and eat out on the screened-in porch. Some evenings they'd go to town to the Hole in the Wall, have a couple of drinks, listen to the jukebox, dance, and share a few laughs with the local crowd. Evenings at the bar began to bore Annette.

Stew would be invited to the Gibson's for dinner, and always enjoyed those evenings. Mr. and Mrs. Gibson were both very fond of Stew. He never saw them that he didn't think about how old and frail Annette's dad was looking. It reminded him of how he missed his own dad.

Stew was always comfortable around them, and they treated him as a part of the family. Mr. Gibson liked to talk of horses and cars and politics. He liked to talk about pranks when he was younger. It made Stew long to be a part of a family. And not just any family, either. This one.

7

HOLE IN THE WALL

When Doug and Irma Sanders got their divorce and Doug put his bar up for sale, Stew bought. He didn't talk a lot about it beforehand. He just went to Doug's house early one Monday morning and said "I can have my attorney draw up the papers this week and give you cash money by next Monday." Doug didn't say a word. Just reached in his pocket, handed Stew the keys. Shook his hand. Walked him out the door.

Stew fell into the habit of opening the Hole in the Wall, serving drinks, stocking the bar, flirting with the girls, laughing along with the customers, and cleaning up at night. The routine became important to him, and he enjoyed his days. The nights got lonely sometimes. Women made passes at him all the time, and he tried not to mix business with pleasure.

Stewart Wilkes was twenty-eight years old, with a fair complexion and a strong chiseled face. His looks were an advantage he hadn't even known he had. Women thought he was handsome with a sparkle in his eyes. Men liked him because he was rugged and easy to be around.

When Stew was sixteen his dark hair was crew cut. His broad shoulders and narrow hips gave him the look of an athlete. His unnaturally large hands were awkward as a teen, yet as he grew into manhood they attained a certain grace. Now his hair had turned almost the color of pewter. More gray than anything. He still had that same light in his eyes that had attracted both males and females since he was a teenager.

The eyes. They were by turns hazel, gray, blue. Stew's eyes were deep like his daddy's. He mesmerized people without even knowing it. Oh, sometimes he was aware of it, though. Sometimes he used it on women. Stewart wasn't a user, but he liked to flirt. He knew if he ever got close enough to look a woman in the eyes she would be fascinated by him. From the eyes he had her if he wanted her. But Stew liked voices and hands. He watched the way women used their hands. Annette's hands were slender, long-fingered, strong, yet delicate and sweet on his face and body.

Annette had been furious with Stew when he bought the bar. Said he lacked ambition and would end up like a bunch of his drunken customers. Occasionally she would stop in during the evening and have a drink, simply to see him and to visit with him. She commented she was busy establishing her practice and didn't have a lot of time. They confined their relationship to an occasional afternoon tryst or Sunday together. Days just went by and went by. He sensed Annette was getting disillusioned with him. He was getting restless with the bar routine, too.

* * *

This particular morning Stew felt lousy. Really lousy. Besides the nausea, there was a heaviness in him. His legs, arms, even his chest felt weighted down. With energy he didn't have he forced himself out of bed, turned on the coffee pot. Went and stood in the shower. Turned both faucets on. Aimed

the showerhead at his chest. Kept turning up
the hot water. Then he turned his body. And
turned. And turned. Made him think of a
chicken on a spit. The water was too hot, but
he could feel it loosening some of the heaviness out of his limbs. He adjusted the tem-
perature. Soaped his body. Opened his
mouth and gargled the hot water. Scrubbed
his scalp until it, too, felt looser. He boomed:
"Hey, Amigo, where did we go,
Days when the rains came
Down in the hollow"

Now his head felt better. His lungs felt
better. His limbs moved. Stew dripped into
the kitchen and poured coffee still mumble
singing:
"Sha la, la..la..la. Sha la, la..la..la.
My brown-eyed girl."

He padded back to his nightstand where
he lit his first Marlboro of the day. He turned
and went back to the shower. Threw a towel
around his neck and shoulders. Bent to pull
on his baggy gray sweatpants and nearly fell
over from the dizziness.
"Whatever happened

To Tuesday and so slow?"

Back into the living room. *"Lah te dah."* Switched the TV on to the morning show. Walked out onto the porch, plopped down on the old sofa, and lit his second Marlboro. He was halfway listening to the TV guy talking about the shape of the universe, when the phone rang. He got up and went back inside.

"Hell-oh-oh."

"Stew, this is Reena."

"Hey, Reena. What's ...".?

"I cain't open up the bar this morning."

"   "Whatsa deal?"

"Well, when I went out to start my car somethin went Zzzzt click click click and then it just went dead."

"Did you call somebody?"

"I'm callin you."

"I mean to look at your car."

"I called Elmer down to the gas station, and he already come and towed it off. The son of a bitch."

"You and Elmer have words?"

"No. I mean the son of a bitch Chevy has cost me nearly four hundred bucks since October. Elmer says this time it looks like the al-turnerator."

Stew grinned at Reena's version of alternator.

"Well, can ya or can'tcha?"

"Can what?" Stew thought now he would have to call Waco and cancel his tests at the V.A. Hospital. He had done so twice, but he also had a business to run. "Reena, why don't I just come pick you up and drop you off on my way outta town?"

"Fine. Oh, just FINE. Then how the hell am I supposed to get back home when my shift is over?"

"Reen, Willy'll be at the bar. Just get him to give you a ride. You know he'll do it."

"Dammit, Stew, you know I won't get in the car with that damn octopus. He's got forty-seven hands and arms and he's always grabbin for stuff."

Stew guffawed. He knew Reena was right, but pushed her a little bit further. "Hell, Reen, by four he'll be too drunk to make a pass at you any. ."

"Damn, Stew. And you want me to get in a car and let him DRIVE? Whatsa matter with you!"

Stew chuckled. "Reena, I'm gonna come pick you up. Take you to the bar. You're gonna open up, work til four. I'm gonna take care of it from there. Settle down. We'll get it taken care of. You hear me?"

"Okay. You . . . I hear you, Stew. But what about getting me home?"

" Honey, did I just tell you I'd take care of it? Stew says he'll take care of you, does he or doesn't he?

"Okay, Stew. Guess I'm just upset about the S.O.B. Chevy. So what time you gonna come get me?"

Stew looked up at the giant lighted clock over his couch. Focused on the mountain stream. 9:14. "I'm practically out the door, Reena. One more thing."

"Yeah, Stew?"

"What stuff?"

"Whaddya mean, what stuff?"

"I mean what stuff does Willy . . ." He laughed and thought he heard her say "Damn you" as she hung up.

* * *

Stew had a little tiny light in the back of his brain that wouldn't go out. It nagged him. He knew he had to get to the hospital for the tests. To find out about the nausea. The skin rash. The weakness. He also knew this time he had to get to the bar *and* make the trip to Waco that he had planned twice before. Something had always come up to make him postpone it. And out of dread, he had always decided the business was more important than the doctor. It had been three months. It was getting worse. He was getting scared.

Stew considered asking Annette to go with him. Asking her would make the trip affirmative, a given; but he wasn't sure he wanted to divulge all this health problems to her just yet. He didn't think he was strong enough to let her see his weaknesses.

8
FULL CIRCLE

Annette's voice was loud, emphatic.

"Dammit, Stew. This is not the way I want to live. I don't need that damned bar every night. I don't want to have to go there just to get a chance to visit with you. Weekend sex may be enough for you, but it's not how I want to spend my life. You need to make some decisions about your own life. Until you decide to get some ambitions beyond bartender, I don't think I can keep seeing you.

He always noticed a voice before anything else about a person. He had never heard Annette's voice raised or strident or cursing. It was unsettling.

He listened to the timbre of people's voices. Stew couldn't bear to listen to a woman with a simpering, high pitched, or whiney voice. Or a man either, for that matter.

He could still hear, in that little pinpoint place in his subconscious, his momma's voice,

Now, remember, Stewart. Sit there til your Daddy gets here.

He recalled Buddy Lloyd's big booming voice, *C'mon Stew, we'll be Viet Nam war buddies, Semper Fi!"*

He could hear the way Reena popped her words out, *That damn octopus. He's always grabbin' for stuff.*

Annette had a sweet, melodious voice. And he loved to listen to her low throaty laugh. Her soft, sweet whispers. *I'll race you to the high meadow.*

He could still recall his daddy's voice reading to him. He never forgot the one about the Lad and Milady.

After he sold the bar, Stew and Annette were married. The first time he read the child song to her, it brought tears to her big brown eyes. From time to time he would take out the little tattered book and read aloud.

This was Stew's world. It was all his. This time, this place, this planet.

CHILD SONG

One old shoe. One old hat.
One little smile,
And that is that.
A pebble, a nail,
A piece of twine;
They all survive the marks of time.

One little sampler. One little doll.
A peppermint,
And that is all.
A curl, a ribbon,
A cup of tea.
What it was will always be.

An impish boy with sandy hair.
A fragile girl with skin so fair.
This is milady. This is me lad.
These are the yesterdays I once had.

Oh, today is singing,
The sun is high
Robins swim and polliwogs fly.
Laugh now milady,
Whistle, me lad.
Tomorrow is soon enough to be sad.

II.

THE LADY NAMED LOU

A STRANGER APPEARS

The wood frame house sat back about a hundred yards from the old blacktop road, and huge oaks and maples lined its driveway. The rich hues of late spring painted the trees. A screened-in porch surrounded three sides of the house with its dark blue shingled roof and dark blue trim. A weathered barn stood just beside and a little to the north of the house. Between the house and barn was a little plot of vegetables, almost overgrown with weeds. A pasture, thick brush, and dense, hilly forest surrounded the back of the property. And a fine peach tree grew around back of the house.

I sat on the screened-in porch rocking. Sitting there shelling peas, I was listening to the sounds of late spring: locusts, birdsong, and an occasional car or truck out on the highway. Lost in thought, I drew my attention to the sound of a vehicle turning into the driveway. It was an old Chevy pickup, shiny bright blue with a visor. I hadn't seen a steering wheel that looked that big for a long time.

Pretty cool. My dog trotted up the drive to meet the vehicle.

I figured this was someone lost, turning around to drive back down the highway the other direction. But the pickup came straight up to the parking grass in front of the house and stopped. A tall man got out, lean, tan, and muscled up, with silver-gray hair peeking out from under his hat. An old beat-up-looking Australian hat with the brim turned up on one side covered his head.

Very cool, I thought to myself. I sat still, watching him until he walked up to the porch.

He finally spoke. "Good afternoon, Ma'am" he said, touching the brim of the hat.

Then I thought, *uh-oh. Too cool.*

I looked straight at him, without moving. "Whatever you're selling, I'm not buying."

He stood there with one foot propped up on the tilted front step. "Oh, Ma'am, you've got me wrong. I'm not selling anythi. . ."

"Are you lost, then?"

"No, Ma'am. I'm just . . ."

"You'd best not try anything funny. Buster here's a pretty good guard dog."

The man stared down at the little Brittany. "Well, if Buster's going to do his fierce watchdog routine, he's waited about three or four minutes too long."

"Well, what *do* you want around here?"

"I stopped by to see if I could get a meal in exchange for a little handyman work."

"I don't need any handy help around here"

The man glanced down at his foot on the broken step.

I was ashamed, thought I'd embarrassed him.

"I can fix you something to eat, though. You can wash up in the tack room out in the barn."

He headed for the barn and hollered back over his shoulder, "Don't care for fried liver, and don't eat much cabbage."

What a nerve! I thought. Aloud "I'll call you."

I went in and got out pork chops. Looked out the kitchen window and saw Buster, stubbed tail wagging, trotting along beside the man. I rinsed off the peas I had just shelled, peeled some potatoes, and started making ice tea. Then I heard sawing and hammering out front. I stepped quickly out to the screened in porch and saw the man nailing new boards on to my front step.

"I told you I don't need handy work in exchange for supper."

"Oh, no trouble, Ma'am. My partner here is doing some fine supervising." Buster was standing, absorbed in watching, his tail intermittently wagging and still.

"You don't have to fix that step. I. . ."
"I didn't want you to fall and break your eggs or something."
"I don't have chickens." I spun on my heels and walked back into the kitchen.

How rude. What does he think I am, some kind of chicken farmer? Did he say egg?
As I finished supper, I tried to ignore what was going on outside, told myself *Be very careful, girl.* I thought about letting him eat out on the porch where there was a nice breeze, then decided that seemed a little silly. I laid out the plates, put the food on the table, and stepped out to call him in for supper. He sat

right there on the porch in MY rocking chair, scratching Buster behind the ears.

"Oh, you startled me!"

"By just sitting here rocking?"

"Well, I mean I was going to call you, and there you were. Didn't know what to call you anyway."

As I started back in to the kitchen, he stood and held out his hand. "Joe Weaver."

I gave his hand a little shake, which turned out very awkward, and moved ahead. When he walked into the house, he removed his hat and laid it on the floor by the door. Buster stood watching him.

"Boy! That smells good! Looks good, too."

"How long has it been since you've eaten?" I asked.

"Oh, I had a good breakfast over at the Silver Spoon in Bird Creek this morning."

"Oh? I thought you were destitute and hungry."

He chewed in silence for a moment. "No, ma'am. I didn't mean to give that impression.

I'm just kind of working my way across country."

"What do you mean 'just kind of'?"

He swallowed. "Lou, I was overseas a while and saw the other guy's country, and when I got home I decided to see a little of my own. What's wrong?"

I sat there startled. "What**ever** possessed you to call me Lou?"

"Well I saw that fancy coffee cup there," he pointed to the little shelf above my sink. "That's not your name?"

I turned and looked. "Oh, yes." I could feel my cheeks burning. The corners of his mouth turned up a little. All my senses were screaming *Watch Out!*

"Now, Lou. May I call you Lou, Lou?"

"Lou, not LuLu."

He went on rambling. I could feel and hear a loud buzzing in my head. I tried not to choke, self-conscious of my own behavior. I gave a slight nod, and for a while the only sounds were the silverware on the dishes and the ice in the glasses.

"You cook a mean pork chop. And I haven't had fresh shelly peas in a l-o-n-g time. Thank you."

"You're welcome, Joe Weaver." I used both names because I thought it sounded a little more reserved, not overly friendly.

"Lou, know what I'd like best to finish up?"

I looked at him dumbly.

"Got any coffee?"

"Oh. Right!" Words came tumbling out of my mouth. "That sounds just perfect. Let's move out to the porch for coffee." *Lou, you're out of your mind.*

He excused himself and went out the door while I brewed a pot of coffee, wondering all the while why I was acting so silly. I got down my LOU cup with the delicate little apples on it and washed it, and poured my coffee into it. *Where did I put my old .22 pistol?*

As we sat and chatted, (I noticed he had left MY rocker for me), Buster lay at Joe Weaver's feet.

"You said you'd been overseas?"

"Yeah. Served in that Asian thing. Came home and decided I'd just start working my way across and around the old US."

"Stay anywhere very long?"

"Naw, find a little work to do, take all kinds of jobs, work until one's finished, then move on. Depends on what interests me."

I kept reminding myself to exercise caution. By turns I'd feel very relaxed and comfortable with this stranger, only to snap out of it and wonder what the hell I was doing. I wanted him gone. I wanted it to be some crazy dream. And then I wanted him to go on talking.

"What does interest you? Isn't there a woman somewhere?" The words just came out of my mouth. I couldn't believe I was asking these personal questions. Yet I was curious to know.

"Yes. When I got out of the service I went back home and married my childhood sweetheart."

"You mean she waited for you?"

Well, not exactly. She got married while I was away, and then divorced. So when I got home she was single again and we got married."

"How romantic, childhood sweethearts!"

"Yeah, it was romantic for about three weeks. Then we found out each other's true nature." He grinned a great big grin and his smile lighting up the darkening porch.

"So what then?" I asked.

"I think we've talked enough about me for a while. What about you?"

"Well, I've never served in the military or been overseas." *Now how do I change the subject?*

He tilted his head back and gave a great belly laugh. "Not too comfortable talking about yourself, huh?"

Then it was my turn to laugh. "I come from the Midwest. Got married right out of high school. Put both of us through college. I found out when we graduated he'd had a cute young blonde student on the side for two years. He was just waiting 'til he got out of school to dump me." I grinned.

"Ouch. Were you devastated?"

"No-o" I chuckled. "I had never really been unhappy; but then when he was gone, I found out I had never really been happy either." *I've never told anyone this in my entire life. Why am I telling this complete stranger?*

We sat in silence listening to the night sounds. I poured more coffee and yawned.

"I guess I'm keeping you up pretty late" he said quietly.

"Well, there's a bunk and stuff in the tack room. I guess you can spend the night there. I don't think it'll be too uncomfortable. I'll just go check it out."

"No. I can take care of myself. Thanks again for the hospitality. Guess I'll see you in the morning?"

"Oh, uh-huh." As Joe Weaver opened the screen door, Buster started after him.

"Buster! You stay here."

The dog and the man both looked back at me. "Please?" he said. Then he and Buster were off to the barn.

When I went in and went to bed, I gave myself a good lecture. *Now Lou, you're behaving recklessly. That man could come in here in the night and slit your throat. And you're treating him like a gentleman caller! And the dog! Buster belongs right out here by my window, where he always sleeps. Ho hum. I'll look for the .22 in the morning.*

* * *

When I awoke, I looked out the bedroom window to see if the pickup was still there. It was. I smelled coffee and walked into the kitchen. *Oh good Lord. He's been in the house while I was asleep.*

As I poured myself a cup, I saw the man through the window. Looked like he was working in the garden plot. I poured another cup of coffee and carried them both out to the porch. I put them on the old wicker table and walked around the side of the house to find him hoeing weeds in the garden. Buster was guarding him.

He looked up. "Mornin," he said.

"I just put coffee on the porch." He removed his hat, wiped sweat off his forehead and followed me around the house, Buster trotting along behind.

"Thanks. I was just waiting for that to brew."

"It's not necessary for you to do that," I said.

"Oh, I've been making coffee since I was a lad."

"I don't mean making coffee, I mean hoeing weeds." *What on earth was he doing coming into the house while I was sleeping? Lou, you are one damn dumb woman.*

"I know I don't *have* to. It just looked like it needed doing." We sipped in silence.

"Don't tell me you carry a hoe around in that pickup?"

He laughed. "Sometime you should take a little tour of your barn. There's all manner of interesting stuff in there. What's with the bunk room?"

"Oh, the man I bought the place from stabled and trained horses and made some bridle trails. Back through the woods behind the pasture in the hills. Trail rides and such. He put in the bunks for helpers."

"What happened?"

"He and his wife moved to Waco to be closer to the V.A. hospital. He was a Viet Nam Veteran, too. Suffered some kind of war syndrome and needed frequent treatments. They were a fine couple. He grew up on this place."

"Well, Buster and I have to get back to work."

He got up and the dog trailed him back out to the garden. I went inside, put on a straw hat and gardening gloves and joined them in the garden. I pulled weeds around the plants while he hoed. All the time I was thinking about what I was doing and how I was going to get him to leave. After all, I did want him to get out didn't I?

We worked side by side. Finally he broke the silence. "You never finished about after he left you."

I was distracted. "Oh?"

"When you got a divorce."

"Oh, that. Well, I applied for a teaching job listed in an education journal. The ad was for a quality high school, rural setting, et cetera, so on a whim I applied. I got it. I taught high school English and American literature here for 38 years. Retired and bought this place two years ago."

"You must have really enjoyed it."

I felt a little wistful.

"Yes, I found out over the years that all students were the same, yet they were all individuals. In every group there were some whose eyes lit up at one thing, some another, some never. But I loved them all." I smiled. "My 'Lou' coffee mug was given to me by a senior from my last graduating class. I imagine he had a crush on Emily Dickinson and got me confused with her." I chuckled.

"Well, I was deeply in love with my high school English teacher, Miss Ada Bridger."

"What was it you so loved about Miss Bridger?"

"She taught me a love of literature and poetry, and a way of looking at things. She called it perspective."

"A true renaissance man. All this," I swept my hand around the newly hoed garden, "and poetry, too." I stared out across the yard.

"The barn and stables seemed to be just a part of the landscape when I moved in. This garden was part of the corral. He had put the shower and bunks in the tack room. I never pay too much attention to it. Cleaned up the bunks and tried to keep the mice and bugs from overtaking it."

"You need a barn kitty."

"No, I need Buster to do his job." At hearing his name, the dog looked up from his nap in the shade. He yawned, and immediately went back to sleep.

"Well, it's a pretty good set up out there if a fella was to need it."

I considered what notion he might be entertaining. "That's hardly germane here."

Leaning on the hoe he threw back his head, showed his pearly whites, and laughed a big belly laugh. I looked up at him.

"Germane? Not gerMANE?" he said. Look out lady, the English teacher is showing."

Hearing us both laugh made Buster finally sit up and wag his tail. I got up, took off my gloves, and started for the house.

He spoke quickly "I didn't mean to offend you."

"No. I'm just through with this conversation." Buster stayed put.

Huh. He's wondering about offending me. Must not want to get off the gravy train. I made sandwiches and ice tea and took them out on the porch. Conversation was minimal as we sat and ate. Buster lazed on the newly re-paired front step.

"Listen, I think I hear grasshoppers."

Joe stopped chewing a second, then said "Just curious, Lou. Who put that garden in?"

"Oh, I poked around here and there and stuck some cucumber and squash seeds in the dirt. Then I decided to get serious and got some tomato plants and planted them."

"Have you ever watered it?"

"Well, it rained a couple of times in April. And in May, I think."

"Have you got a hose?"

I snapped at him. "I suppose if you look in the barn you'll find whatever you want.

You haven't seemed to have any trouble so far. And it looks like the peach tree could use some water, too."

We sat a little longer in silence, listening to the grasshoppers rasping.

"So, after 40 years here haven't there been suitors?"

I laughed out loud. *Back to that, huh?* "Well, once a school bus driver took me out to dinner." *Why do I keep falling into these conversation traps?*

After a pause when I didn't continue, "So what then?"

"We ate," I laughed.

"You sure enough sound like an old maid school teacher. Nobody else in all these years?"

I paused, giving this some thought. *Lou, keep your mouth shut.* "Well, the mailman got kind of sweet on me after his wife passed away."

"And?"

Lord, please slap your hand over my mouth. I feel like a wind up toy. Let me run down, God, please.

"I know better than to get wound up, uh, get involved with a recent widower." I got up.

He didn't let it drop. 'Well, so how does it stand now?"

I ignored the question.

"I have things to do." I went into the house.

* * *

Those first few days passed easily. I worked in the garden some, read some, and cooked meals for us. Buster would follow the man around during the day, guard him as he did little chores, and follow him to his bunk at night. I was a little jealous that Buster seemed to like him so much. Each night I pondered the situation.

What are you doing, Lou? Do you expect this to lead somewhere? What do you think he's after?

And the next night the self-talk would continue.

Lou, are you going to ask him to leave? Or how long he plans to stay? What in the world do you plan to do?

Joe cleaned and rearranged the stalls in the barn. Kept up the hoeing and watering in the garden, and fixed any little thing he could find to fix. Late one morning, "Would you like to come and see what I've done in the barn?"

I followed him with Buster trotting along, panting in great anticipation. It was almost as if the dog was saying, "Wait'll you see what we've done!" When I stepped into the barn from the bright sun, all I could see was the dust motes dancing in the shafts of light. As my eyes adjusted to the dimness, I gasped. I walked past each stall, one with hoes, rakes, garden tools, water hose all coiled up, a ladder, all sorts of tools and equipment all neatly arranged. .Stalls swept clean.

"My word! Where did you get all this stuff?"

The belly laugh. "Lady, it was all right here. Just kind of scattered around. Look at this next one." The wooden gate had a little metal plaque on it that had been recently shined. It was engraved "Chugger."

"I wonder what that's about?" I said, half to myself.

"Somebody's favorite pony I expect."

In that stall were an old television, a window fan, wooden table, and cans of rusty nails, bolts, and metal stuff I didn't recognize. Again, floor swept clean. He showed me around wordlessly.

Across the aisle along the other wall, another stall. This one had lots of old, worn tack hanging on the walls and a row of big metal garbage cans with lids, and what looked like a workbench built against the back wall.

"My goodness!"

"What do you think?" he asked.

"I think what would anyone want with all those trash cans?"

He laughed. "I believe they were for feed storage. Anyway that's what I thought when I found all that grain in the bottom of the cans."

We both laughed.

"Joe Weaver, you've done a terrific job. I don't know how to thank you."

"Well . . ."

Oh no, I thought, here it comes. "Yes?"

"Well, I have several things I'd like to do, and if I could bunk out here a spell, I'd like to stick around until I get some things done."

He was forcing me to make a decision, and I didn't want to. "Like what?"

"Well, for starters, I'd like to put a coat of paint on this barn before it gets too rotten and weathered and falls down. I'd like to stay and see the garden bear. I really like fresh tomatoes, you know. And peaches, too. And I'd like to take a look at the bridle trails and see what needs to be done there. Then . . ."

"Stop," my voice sounded harsh. "Joe Weaver, I don't have the money to paint this barn. I'm. . "

"I'm not asking for money. Let me finish."

"It sounds like you intend to become a long-term resident, and I'm not looking for anything permanent. I'll decide when and how to get the barn painted, when to pick the tomatoes, and when, if ever, the hiking trails need to be looked after. And when to go fishing, and," my voice rising with each breath, "and when Buster gets to run after somebody else."

"You like to fish, too?"

We were both silent for a moment.

"Now are you finished?" We stood there in the darkened barn. I couldn't look at him so I looked down at my feet, almost crying.

"I have a little plan, and I'd like to tell you about it if you want to hear me out."

"I'm hot. I just want to sit down."

He quickly took my arm and led me to his bunkroom, opened the door, and steered me to the chair by the little wooden table.

"Lou, without imposing anything on you, these are just things I want to do because I like you. And Buster. I'd like to go to Yancey Crossing and get some paint, some fertilizer, and a few more things."

He turned and walked out. I could hear water running. Within a few seconds he was back with a wet washcloth.

"Here, put this on the back of your neck or on your forehead or something."

I put the damp cloth on my forehead. It felt cool. I felt calmer.

"What things?"

"I need to do some wiring to repair the fan back there. It's getting pretty stifling in here at night. I need a couple of tools, and some man stuff."

"What man stuff?"

"We'll never get anywhere if you keep interrupting me. So happens I need some personal hygiene items."

"Hygiene items? Well, good grief, Joe Weaver, I've got soap and shampoo. All you have to do... "

He always thought it was a good sign when she called him by both names. It made him feel he mattered.

"Don't talk to me about money. Don't talk to me about who can afford what. Talk to me about whether or not you'd like to have these things done. And whether or not you'd like to have my company around long enough to get them done." He paused. "Now you can talk."

"Yes."

"Yes to what?"

"Yes, I'd like for you to stay and get some things done. Yes, I'd like for you to have home grown tomatoes with me. Yes to all of it. One caveat."

"Caveat?" Under his breath, "Oh hell, now its caveats."

"I'm very serious, Joe Weaver. I like your company. I respect you. You're easy to be around. I'm not looking for anything permanent or intimate. The Lord only knows why, but I trust you. Your friendship would mean a lot to me, but that's as far as it goes." *There. I said it. If I could just make myself ask when he's leaving. What his ulterior motives are. Whatthehell he thinks he's doing around here.* He interrupted my thoughts.

"Lady, I feel the same way. But I think it's a bit arrogant for to you think I have ulterior motives. Now go wash your face. We're going to town so I can do a little tradin."

I rose from the chair and headed for the house. *Well, I do need a few groceries.*

The ride to Yancey Crossing was comfortable and easy. I asked about his pickup.

"It was Dad's. Mom died while I was in the service, and I got it when Dad sold the farm. Restored it myself."

I could tell he was quite proud of that.

I told about starring in a play when Bird Creek started up a little theater group.

"What play?"

"Auntie Mame."

He grinned. "Bird Creek wasn't ready for that, were they?"

"Hardly." I laughed so hard it brought tears to my eyes.

Joe enjoyed the laughter and joined in.

In Yancey Crossing I told him he could drop me off at the grocery store while he did his shopping.

"No Ma'am. This is a joint venture. I'm going to stop by the bank for an errand."

"But. . ."

"This isn't a "But," Lou. This is our agenda. When I get out of the bank we'll go to the home improvement store, and you can pick out the paint you want on the barn."

"Pick out red paint?"

"It's your barn. Pick purple if you want to. And as I was saying, I'll get a couple of tools and some hardware, some fertilizer. Then we'll go grocery shopping together. I might want something for me. Then we'll go to the drugstore, and I can get my personal stuff."

"Here's where I put *my* foot down," I said. "We can get groceries and any other things at SuperMart. Just one stop."

"Just can't leave it alone, can you? And when the shopping's done, I'm taking you out to dinner."

"Then what?"

"We eat" he grinned.

When we drove into town, Joe drove straight to the bank. "Do you need to go in?" he asked.

"No, thanks." I sat with the window rolled down and absent mindedly thought about where he got his money and how he got an account here. Something didn't fit right. It didn't take very long, and he was back.

Hopping into the pickup, he said, "There. That's done. In case you're wondering where I get my money ..."

"Oh no," I lied.

He went on. "I was the only heir to Daddy's farm; I've got my military retirement, an IRA, and the occasional job. The bank back home handles it all for me. Sends it to me wherever I am."

"Just like that?"

"Yeah, just like that; there's a little paperwork, but it all works out great for me."

Why is he telling me all this? "Now I suppose you'll be wanting to know what I live on?"

"Wouldn't dream of asking."

We drove on to the home improvement center, and he went off to look at things. I meandered around, fascinated by all the gadgets and doodads. Saw a hanging planter with red petunias, went back and got a shopping cart and put the flowers in it. As I wandered around the checkout counter, he showed up with his cart filled with stuff.

"Come" he said "we'll look at paint." I meekly followed him to the paint department and was blown away by the huge selection of paint colors.

"Oh my word, you can't expect me to pick a color from all this."

"No, Lou, down here are the paints suitable for painting a barn. You can pick from these."

"Red."

"Would you at least look at them?"

"Well, this looks like a nice barny red," I'd said, pointing at the first one that caught my eye. "What do you think?"

"BARNy? I think it's a terrific barny red. I'll check out then we'll drive around back and pick up the paint.

I walked back out to the pickup and set the petunias inside on the floorboard. The pickup bed seemed to be full of . . . junk. He came out, loaded his things into the back, returned the shopping cart and got in.

"Oh, pretty flowers. You could have put them in the back."

"I felt like they were safer in here with me."

He laughed as he drove around back where two guys loaded the paint cans and some lumber.

"Now, on to SuperMart."

He found a parking spot in the crowded lot, jumped out, ran around, opened the door, and held out his hand.

When we got inside he grabbed a cart, and I stepped in behind him and grabbed my own cart.

"Let's just do this all in one basket."

"Too hard to separate," I said. "I need to pay for my own stuff."

"No" he said, "this will all go together. I intend to get what I want, you can get what you want, and we'll check out together. I'm paying. No fuss or I'll cause a really big scene. Believe me, you don't want to see that. Remember, it's payday for me."

There was that big beautiful white-toothed grin. How could I refuse?

We strolled up and down the aisles; some toothpaste and shaving cream for him; hand lotion and shampoo for me. He steered me toward clothing and tried on a billed cap.

"Want one?" he said as he plopped a ladies floppy hat on my head.

"Joe Weaver, I have a straw hat." I felt myself flush as he stood back and eyeballed me. "No, I think this is the one" as he swooped that one off and put a big yellow straw hat on my head.

"How could anyone resist you, or the straw hat?"

"People are s-t-a-r-ing," I sang in a low voice. He tried steering me over toward the grocery section. I stood rooted.

"Oh for God's sake, Lou."

He reached up and pulled the hat off my head and put it on his. I cracked up. Then he pulled the hat off and put it on top of the things in the basket.

When we went to the grocery section, I picked up butter, eggs, milk, a chuck roast, and some chicken. Then some dog chow. He went down aisles seeming to throw everything he looked at into the cart. He picked out steaks, frozen shrimp, weenies, cans and cans of things. Cookies. Everything.

I tried to keep my voice down. "My goodness, Joe Weaver, there are only two of us. What are you planning on doing with all this food?" I was thinking *Lou, he thinks he's staying. What are you planning on doing about it?*

"Variety, girl, variety. Didn't I see a deepfreeze on that eastside porch?"

"Yes, but I don't even know if it works."

"It will."

When we checked out, he maneuvered himself around so that I couldn't tell what the bill was. *Don't worry, Lou. Let him afford what he wants.* Driving out of the parking lot he started east.

"Where now?"

"I told you I'd take you out to dinner, and that's what I intend to do."

"NO! I'm putting my foot down again, Joe Weaver. We have milk and eggs, not to mention the ice cream I saw you put in there. We need to get back before this stuff starts melting."

"Well, that settles it. We wouldn't want the eggs to melt. And I've got to keep an eye out for that foot, don't I?"

"You know what I mean."

When they got home Buster hopped, ran and circled around their legs. The man reached down and scratched the dog's ears as he started carrying in the groceries. He set the potted petunias on the porch. He started to try and help put the groceries up.

"Just get out of my way. You and Buster go do your thing."

I put the groceries away, stuffing and shuffling around to try to make everything fit in the cupboards, refrigerator, and freezer compartment. I heard scraping and clinking outside. Every now and then I saw the top of his hat pop up outside the window. I tried not to look, tried not to think about it.

Finally, I fixed hotdogs and a pitcher of tea and took it out on the porch. I walked around the side and saw he had wires and thingies strewn all over.

"Are you ready for something to eat?"

"Could you give me about ten minutes to get this thing back together."

"Sure."

I sat down and sipped my tea. I could hear him talking under his breath to Buster.

"That should fit right there. Yeah. See Buster? Oh, perfect. We need to tighten this up a little more. Think you could help me lift this thing back in there? Oh, okay then, you supervise."

Thud. Scrape.

"Unhh. Hah!" "Done, buddy." He walked past me out the door and to the bunk room.

When he and Buster came trotting back to the house, he had washed his face and hands, taken off his hat, and combed his hair.

"Sorry I made you wait. Just wanted to be sure I got the freezer working before I put it back together."

He pulled out a chair and sat down to a plate of hot dogs with mustard, chili, relish, onions, some tea, and some sliced tomatoes.

"Yum. Good food."

Good grief. He acts like everything I fix is fine cuisine. Trying to ingratiate himself with me. Huh.

"So it's fixed? I thought a belt was something on a car."

"See, that's why you need my help. You can start using it anytime, but it looks like it needs washing down inside."

The hell I need his help. I could have done that. Probably. With the right tools. Buster could have shown me just as well as him.

"I'll have to do that tomorrow. Right now I'm tired, and I want to get some reading done before I go to bed."

"Reading some great romance novel to put you to sleep?"

"Hardly. My Sunday school lesson, and scriptures for Sunday."

"Tomorrow's Sunday? You go to church?"

In my best schoolteacher voice: "Today is Saturday. I need to get started on the lesson for Sunday. Which is tomorrow."

Silence.

"What time is church?"

'"Oh. It starts at eleven. Would you like to go with me?" *Oh, Lord. I can't believe I said that. What if he takes me up on it?*

"What church is it?"

"Are you sure you want to face that?" I asked.

"Lou, are you afraid I'll embarrass you?"

"No, I'm afraid it will start gossip I can't handle."

He laughed. "That gossip's been going on for years. You just haven't been aware of it. It's what keeps towns this size going. What time shall I be ready in the morning?"

"Bird Creek Methodist. I'll leave about twenty minutes til."

"What about Sunday School?"

"I know I can't handle that."

I got up, went in and cleaned the kitchen, and started for my bedroom. He had come in from the porch and was right behind me. It startled me to realize he was so close to me and my bedroom.

I stifled a yawn. "Please shut the front door on the way out."

The man went out to the bunkhouse, hit the sack and spoke in the dark to the dog.

"Ya know, Buster. This is a good life." Buster huffed. "I feel necessary, like I belong. Never can figure women, can ya?" He heard Buster snoring softly.

Next morning Lou rose and got ready for church. She looked in the full length mirror and saw good breasts, sagging butt, wrinkled skin. *I need to take better care of myself. I need a new girdle.*

She chose the blue silk pantsuit, and low-heeled leather sandals. As she put on make-up, she appraised her features. The hair was silver-streaked, cut short. Cheekbones prominent, mouth wide. *Regal*, she thought. The face was wrinkled, especially around the eyes and mouth. *Laugh lines*, she decided.

When she walked into the kitchen, she was startled to see the back of the man's legs, standing on a stool on the east porch. She craned her neck around the left to the window and saw that he was hanging her petunias. She poured coffee and carried it out.

He couldn't see her around the corner, but she heard "Good morning. Coffee smells good."

When he stepped down off the stool and came around the corner of the porch, he stopped dead in his tracks. She hardly recognized him in his good clothes.

"Well" he said, "you look nice."

"Thank you. You too." *It's been a long time since anyone cared how I looked. God, please don't let me blush.*

He grinned and she handed him his coffee. He sipped and they laughed simultaneously.

"What's so funny to you?" she asked.

"Same thing as you. All this quality time around one another, and we've never seen each other dressed. Up, I mean. All dressed up."

It sounded like he was implying something and she ignored him. "Would you like some breakfast?"

"No. Today's the day I'm taking you out to eat. We're dressed up, don't have a pickup full of stuff, not tired from shopping, no groceries to get home."

"Okay, okay, yes."

* * *

As we pulled into the gravel parking lot at Bird Creek Methodist, people quit visiting and turned to look at us. Some who weren't even visiting just stopped and stared.

"They're looking at my truck."

I laughed out loud. We hung back a little and walked into the church just as the organ started playing. He followed me down to the middle, near the front where I always sat. As the choir filed in some of them turned their heads to look directly at him.

I found out he had a beautiful singing voice, knew the hymns, and followed the message closely. The sermon was based on First Corinthians 1, and Reverend Nelson did a fine job. Didn't raise his voice too many times. Didn't bang his fist on the lectern at all. The sunlight through the stained glass windows shown amber and emerald on my hymnal and around me. I felt as if God was making his face to shine upon me.

After the service we made our way out front, shook hands with Reverend Nelson, who welcomed Joe Weaver profusely but didn't ask his name. As we stepped down the front steps, it seemed like the entire church stood in line to introduce themselves to Joe Weaver and welcome him. He'd say "Joe, friend of Lou's, glad to meet you." "Thank you," and so on until it came to Clara Miller.

"Lou, I didn't know you had any relatives."

"Clara, I'd like for you to meet my friend, Joe."

"Joe, any friend of Lou's is a friend of ours. Why don't you and Lou come over for Sunday dinner with Ben and me?"

"Well, thank you, Miss Clara, but we already have plans." As he turned to go, I could see the corners of his mouth turning up. I heard Clara mutter "Well. We *all* need a friend like that."

I spun around and spoke loudly and clearly, "Don't you wish, Clara Miller, don't you wish."

By the time the man helped me into the pickup and closed the door, we were both laughing.

You don't have to make enemies just because you feel defensive. Especially Clara Miller. Her tongue could outrun a Singer showing machine any day of the week. I laughed again. Joe just looked over at me.

He drove to the Rustic Inn Steakhouse and helped me out of the pickup. When we got inside there was a line. The attendant asked "Two?" Joe gave a nod of his head. "Sir, it will be a few minutes. Would you like to wait in the lounge?"

Before I could say anything, a server appeared and led us to the bar. When we were seated, Joe gave the waiter our order.

"Two vodka gimlets."

I started to protest.

"Don't worry," he said. "I won't let you get drunk and take advantage of me."

We relaxed over the drinks and made easy small talk about the church service, the curiosity of the people, the garden. Soon the waiter was back to lead us to a table.

"May we be served in here where it's quiet?" Joe asked.

"Certainly. I'll have a server come take your order. Another drink?"

"No, thank you" I responded quickly.

"When the server came, Joe said, "May I order for you?" I nodded. He ordered salmon poached in white wine, gratin potatoes, and spinach vinaigrette.

"I didn't know how hungry I was til I heard you say all that."

While we were still sipping our drinks, a man walked into the lounge, up to the bar and ordered something. He turned to go back to his table and spied us.

"Miz Lou!" he said "How you doing?" He was looking straight at Joe Weaver when he said this.

"Very well, thank you, Larry. This is my friend Joe Weaver."

"No, don't get up" Larry said, reaching out and shaking Joe's hand   "It's nice to meet you, Joe.   Lou, you're looking beautiful as ever." He turned and left.

"Well, the cat's out of the bag" I said.

"What cat? What bag?"

"You know darned well what I'm talking about, Joe Weaver. That was the superintendent of schools. Larry Taver's as big a gossip as any woman ever could be."

He laughed. The waiter appeared with the food. "Will there be anything else?" I asked for ice water, and Joe ordered coffee. We were both making little "uum and ahh" noises over our food when a heavily made-up redhead with flashy jewelry tottered up to the table.

.   "Lou, you rashcal," she slurred. "Larry said you had a boyfriend."

"Marge, this is my friend Joe."

"Well, Joe, are you living with our little LouLou?" She batted her heavily mascared eyelashes at him. He grinned.

"No, Marge, I'm doing some work out at her place."

As she turned to go she almost lost her balance. She said suggestively, "Well, when you finish there, I need some things done at my place, too."

As she left, I said under my breath "Pull in your claws, Marge Taver."

This time Joe Weaver guffawed, raised his eyebrows and said, "Oh, that cat. That bag was pretty soaked." And we both had grins over that.

Before we could finish the salmon, three or four people just happened to come into the bar, not drinking just looking around. Some stopped by our table; some just came by for a good look. When we had eaten our meal, Joe ordered coffee for both of us. We sipped in peace and silence.

"You ready to blow this joint?"

"Ten minutes ago" I sighed.

* * *

Days slid by. We worked in the yard. He would clatter and bang around in the barn, then stop for a break and have some tea. We would both talk about what each of us had gotten done. At first I worried about impropriety. Then I began to relax. I found I enjoyed the rhythm of things, the routine that so quickly became my routine.

One afternoon as we sat on the shady porch, the mailman turned into the drive.

"Looks like you're getting a special delivery."

"No, it's Alec checking up on you."

Alec drove up and parked under the big maple, then got out with some mail in his hand.

"Hey, Miz Lou."

"Hi, Alec. What have you got for me?"

Without looking at the mail in his hand, he said it looked like a flyer for new storm windows, something from the insurance man, and he couldn't tell what it was from the state. He handed the mail to me and looked at Joe. Said "I guess you'd be that drifter been hanging around out here?"

"Guess so" Joe said, staring right back at Alec.

I got up. "Thanks for the mail, Alec. Tell Cora Jane I said hi." Then I walked into the house, my pulse a little more rapid than usual.

Joe and Buster just sat there. At last Alec hollered "Call me if you need anything, Miz Lou." Then he went back to his truck and drove off. Before he could clear the driveway, I was back out on the porch.

Joe Weaver tried to sound casual. "So who's Cora Jane?"

"She's Alec's sister. She's lived with him since his wife died." Joe just kept looking toward the driveway.

* * *

When Joe Weaver started painting the barn, I noticed he had repaired the wooden ladder and rigged up a scaffold. When he was getting all his stuff ready, I walked over from the garden and said, "I wondered what you got that rope for."

"Scaffold."

I went back to my gardening chores, and pretty soon heard him singing in his beautiful baritone voice:

Welcome to my world. Won't you come on in, Miracles I guess, still happen now and then.

"Joe, that's lovely."

I'll be waiting there, with my arms unfurled

122

waiting just for you, Welcome to my world.

He looked from his perch on the ladder and hummed as he started down.

Hum-Hum-Hum, hum-hum,
the key to this heart of mine.

"Eddy Arnold," I said.

"Jim Reeves," he said.

"I started to say that."

When he reached the bottom, he grabbed me and swung me around, and started dancing across the yard, still humming and singing. I felt like an idiot and tried to resist, but after a moment, I relaxed and became a feather floating in his arms, humming along. I liked the feel of his strong muscular chest, his big hand around my waist.

"Joe Weaver, where I come from they'd call you a troubadour." I pulled away and headed for the porch.

"Lou, where I come from, you're an old maid schoolteacher."

I laughed. He followed me to the porch.

"By the way, I noticed the entire countryside calls you Miz Lou. What did your students call you?"

"Miz Whidbey."

"Whidbey? I had no idea."

"That's because Alec won't let you look at the mail." I got a huge bang out of that and laughed hard. Joe didn't see the humor in it.

"Seriously, I liked holding you in my arms and dancing. It felt really good."

"Now, you hold on, Joe Weaver. I've told you before I'm not in the market for a partner of **any** kind."

"Good gawd, Lou, I'm not talking about *intimacy*. I'm talking about two people holding on to each other and moving around the floor to music! It's called dancing. You're good at it."

"Well, yes, I used to like to dance."

"I was thinking maybe sometime we could drive in to the VFW for the Saturday night dance. After all, the cat's out of the bag."

"Okay" I said, with a yearning inside.

We did go dancing on Saturday night. A couple of people stopped by our table to say hello. Women flirted with Joe Weaver. A short, sweaty fat man asked me to dance. I accepted and found he was quite a good dancer. Joe and I danced several, a couple of fast ones and two or three slow dances. It felt heavenly. Marge Taver stopped by and tried to get Joe to dance with her. She was staggering, and Joe made an excuse. A former teacher stopped by and introduced himself to Joe, and said to me, "Miz Whidbey, does Alec know you can dance like that?"

The music was good. We danced and laughed and danced. We both had a great time. I thought.

On the way home Joe said "Do you have to check in with Alec when you go out dancing or on a date?"

This really annoyed me and made me feel somehow like I was two-timing somebody.

"Certainly not. I'm an independent woman and don't have to check with anyone about what I do or want to do. And that includes you."

Why did I think I had to add that? And in that tone of voice?

Silence.

Finally, "Miz Lou, all that dancing and talking tired me out. Can we skip church in the morning?"

"Oh, no you don't, Joe Weaver. "

He chuckled. And sang louder than anyone else on Sunday morning.

BLACKBERRY SUMMER

As the weather turned hotter, we picked in the garden, puttered around the yard, walked the bridle trails. I wore my yellow straw hat. We found blackberries.

"Great!" he said, "Let's pick 'em."

"We don't have anything to put them in."

"Your big straw hat would be just right." he said.

"Oh no! Blackberries would stain my hat."

He reached over, snatched the hat off my head and started picking berries and dropping them in. I was furious. It was *my* hat after all. Even if he did buy it for me. I stood motionless and angry. He seemed to be unaware of my irritation.

After a few silent moments, while he continued to pick, he said softly, "I'll buy you another."

As we picked, the chatter started up again. Both of us started sneaking big, fat, juicy berries into our mouths. He grinned and said, "Lucky you've got a big head."

We got my hat full and his hat full. Then we made our way back to the house in the heat of the day, with purple fingers, stained hats. We cooled off on the porch drinking tea and dipping berries in sugar and eating them.

We went back up the trail next day and chopped some brush and got the rest of the berries. Buster hunted grasshoppers and mischief.

For dinner that night we had sliced tomatoes, T-bone steaks, and blackberry cobbler. We were all three in high spirits.

* * *

I became more and more dependent on Joe's companionship and presence. One evening after our grocery-shopping trip to town, he helped me unload groceries and put things in the freezer he had fixed. Then he said "Oh, look here. One more thing. And he opened a box with a birthday cake that had "Happy Birthday Miz Lou" written on it.

"Joe Weaver! When did you do that?"

"I ordered it before we went to town. On the phone. Your phone, there,'" he pointed. "I never see you use it or hear Alec call you or anything.

I frowned. "Mister, it's **not** my birthday." *Why in the world was he bringing up Alec?*

"Sure it is. Your birthday is when somebody gives you a birthday cake."

"And sings Happy Birthday?" I grinned. "You didn't happen to sneak any ice cream in there, too, did you?"

"Vanilla for you, butter pecan for me." We skipped supper and dug into ice cream and cake. He sang Happy Birthday. Buster joined in.

* * *

A few mornings later, I awoke to the smell of coffee. I rose, dressed, and went to the kitchen. The man was sitting at the table, scratching Buster's ear with one hand and sipping his coffee with the other. He looked up at me. I got a very funny feeling in the pit of my stomach, knew something unpleasant was coming.

"Thank you for the coffee, Joe. What's up?"

"Miz Lou, I'm taking a little trip. I'd be glad to take you with me, but I don't know exactly how long I'll be gone."

Silence.

Finally, "May I ask where you're going? And why?"

He grinned at me, and his eyes were gentle. "Don't worry, Miz Lou. I'm not pissed off or running away. Every year around this time a bunch of old buddies from my unit gather for a little reunion. I'd even ask you to go with me, but besides the fact I think you'd say "no," there'll be some strong language, strong drink and et cetera.

I looked at him quizzically "I don't understand. What's et cetera? How did you hear about this? How long have you known? Where do you go? How long . . ."

He reached over and placed his hand over mine on the table.

"Hey there, slow down. No cause for alarm. I'm going to explain, if you'll just give me time."

I jerked my hand out from under his. He sat straighter in his chair.

"Every year when we meet, it's planned where we'll meet the next year. This year it's Red River, New Mexico. We eat, drink, tell war stories, lies, cry some tears, drink some more. You know, guy stuff."

"No, I don't know. When will you be leaving?"

"It's always the last week of August."

"JOE WEAVER! That's now! Don't you think you might have talked to me about it a little sooner? You couldn't have let me know?"

"Why? Did we have plans?" He almost bit his tongue.

"Don't be flippant. You know I depend on you. Your . . .

"For what?"

"For one thing I've changed my whole" I let my voice drop off. Then tried again. "We talked about your joining the choir. We . . . How long will you be gone?"

"Well, see, that's the thing, Lou. I don't know. I've never been to New Mexico. There's some things I'd like to see and do.

Things to sort out." He paused. "Maybe you should sort out things, too."

My voice was now low and even. "Oh, please. Don't try to placate me with your talk. I know you have an entire existence that doesn't include me." My voice started rising again. "I've told you repeatedly I have no attachment to you." *Something was building inside me. Rage? Panic? Fear.*

"I might find a job as a ski instructor," he said grinning. "After the reunion I might have you come meet me, and we'd see some things together."

"No, I will not come meet you. Have you explained all this to Buster?"

He laughed and I burst into tears, left the room, and shut myself in my bedroom. As soon as I closed the door, I felt like a fool. I was embarrassed by my behavior. *After all, Told him from the beginning, "No attachments." Now, I'd let him see me cry. Oh, Lord, give me strength.* I got myself together, went out to the screened in porch and started watering my plant. My heart hurt.

I listened closely, but heard very little from the bunkroom. An occasional thud or banging sound made me listen more intently. I wasn't concentrating on what I was doing, drowned my petunia plant and poured water all over the front of my slacks.

After a while the man came out of the barn, Buster trailing behind. He put a load of things in his pickup.

I gave up concentrating and just sat down on the porch and watched. All the energy seemed drained from my bones. When he noticed me sitting there, he came up to the porch and sat down across from me.

"Listen, Lou" he started.

"Joe Weaver, just let it go. Let it go. I embarrassed myself by raising my voice like that, and getting so upset and emotional. We have no ties. It just caught me by surprise, that's all. You know I don't care what you have to do." This all came out in one, jumbled burst.

"Ouch. That smarts."

"Joe. I imagine it does. Your free lifestyle has my blessing. I think it's one of the things I …one of the things I admire about you. Now, you tell me what I need to do to make things easier for you."

*Like, put cayenne pepper in that coffee, you snake. And make your eyes water. And burn the back of your throat. Make **you** cry.* I squelched my thoughts.

We got it all worked out, and both agreed, no matter what he did, he could keep some of his tools and things in the barn as long as he wanted. I instructed him on phone calls and letters if he needed me to do anything. He agreed to keep in touch so I would at least know what part of the country he was in. I agreed, with a grin, to explain things to Buster. *But I was angry. Really angry. Or maybe I just had hurt feelings. False pride? Ego? Oh damn. I felt broken.*

LOU'S STORY

The next morning when I awoke, I glanced out the window to see that the pickup was gone. I ran barefoot into the yard, across to the barn, only to look in and see the empty bunkroom.

"Oh, damn you" I sobbed, "You left without even saying goodbye." I walked back into the house, Buster slumping along behind. I went in and slipped on my housecoat, my slippers. Went into the kitchen, made coffee, took it out to the porch, and sat there, numb. I don't know how long. The coffee got cold.

Finally. *Oh that's enough, Lou. Get up, and get over it.*

* * *

I started by cleaning out the refrigerator. Days went by. I cleaned out the cupboards. I went to church. *Oops.*

"Where's Joe?"

"Alec said Joe's pickup's not there any-more.'

"Did you run Joe off?"

I should have known it would happen. We were thought of as a couple, and people were curious to know what happened. They, too, missed Joe Weaver, just as I did. But I didn't let on; couldn't turn loose with any explanation without getting choked up.

I said, "Oh, he had to make a trip." Or "He's traveling right now." Or something really inane like "Oh, you know. Duty calls." Sometimes I'd just act like I didn't hear the comments and questions.

As the days went by, they quit asking, and my life settled back into the former routine. Except for the gaping hole inside me. I continued to do little busy work around the house. Made blackberry jelly. Cried over it. Took Buster for hikes in the forest and hills. Went to church. And read. I read book after book. I discovered some authors and revisited old favorites. I read thrilling stories that I couldn't even remember when I closed the book. I wore the yellow straw hat with the big purple splotches on it. Sometimes even wore it around the house when I was reading, or cooking.

The man never wrote. He didn't call. I'd had the feeling he wouldn't when we discussed it. I had no idea where he was. *It was all a big fat lie,* I told myself and would get angry all over again. I cried. I got mad. I got sad. I cried some more. I wanted the hurt to stop.

I cleaned out the bunkroom. Redecorated it in my own way by adding new sheets and spreads on the bunks. Got Clay and Penny, from down the road, to go to an auction with me. They helped me get the things home and unloaded. I got a decent desk and chair, a recliner and a wardrobe closet. That made the room seem very small. I moved the old things to another stall. I sweated, got dirty, and went to bed tired every night. In my frenzy of cleaning, I tidied up all the stalls, or pretended to. Joe really hadn't left anything untidy. When I would come to some of his tools, I would look at them, finger them protectively. And go right on. Buster assisted with his usual enthusiasm. His snoring helped me keep up the rhythm and pace. A couple of times I found myself singing. *Atta girl. Louder. Blow the rafters off.* Buster felt better when I was vocal. So did I. Some days I would see just how loud I could sing. And how complex a conversation I could get into with Buster. Some days I thought I was going insane. So did Buster.

Once in a while a neighbor or some teacher would come to visit. It was mostly out of curiosity. But they were kind so I learned to deal with the company. Penney would call periodically to check on me. I really liked Penney and took them blackberry jam and a cake or pie now and then. We'd have coffee and visit.

At last Alec quit calling. After all my rejections and rebuffs, the old fool finally got the idea. I guess. Or maybe he'd found some other old gray-haired lady to annoy.

Sometimes a former student would drop by to visit and tell me about his or her dreams and plans; and thank me for my guidance. These visits gave me a great deal of pride and pleasure.

* * *

One evening Penney called and invited Lou over for Saturday night supper.

"Oh, I'd like that Penney. What can I bring?"

"Nothing but your charming smile, Lou. We've also invited a friend of Clay's, too. We think you might like him."

I swallowed, hard. "Oh, I don't know, Penney, I'm . . ."

"Lou Whidbey, this is supper. If you like him fine. If you don't, fine. It's just supper! Wouldn't you like somebody else's cooking for a change?"

I laughed. "Yes, okay, Penney."

"Shall I have him come by and pick you up?"

"No, definitely not."

I was a little nervous about the whole idea of a blind date, but Penney was right. And I also enjoyed Clay and Penney's company.

On Saturday night I put on very little makeup, wore slacks and a plaid shirt, and tried not to look too prissy. Just as long as he's not an insurance salesman, I laughed to my-self.

When I arrived, Penney met me at the door with Clay and his friend right behind.

"Lou, this is our friend, Ed."

Ed? I thought of Art Carney and Ed Norton, the plumber and giggled nervously.

"Hello, Lou. Pleased to meet you." We shook hands and all filed into the living room. I sat on the end of the couch and Ed sat in a chair right next to me. He would lean forward and smile at me as we talked. Clay and Penney both went to the kitchen to finish preparing dinner.

"And what does a pretty girl like you do?" Ed asked.

Pretty girl? I thought. *Oh, bore.* "Oh, I garden" I said, "and just routine things that old girls like me do. And you?"

I had noticed that he wasn't bad looking. Except that coal-black mop on his head. It was one of the worst toupees I had ever seen. I tried to keep from staring. And giggling.

"Me? I'm in the insurance game."

Then it all gave way. I laughed out loud.

He looked offended, and then grinned.

"I see you've heard about us wild boys in the insurance industry."

I tried to get hold of myself. "It's just that as a child I always dreamed of growing up and meeting an insurance man."

"Well," Ed smiled "you got him!"

God sent Clay and Penney in at that very moment to announce dinner. We all made small talk, Ed a little too much, a little too small. When dinner was over, Penney said, "Let's all move to the living room."

I saw my chance. "I'll help you clean up here, and then I need to go home." Penney looked at me with a pleading look.

"No, Clay will help me clean up later. Do you really have to go?"

Ed and Clay overheard this exchange and Ed jumped in. "I'll be glad to see you home."

"No, thank you. I have my car. Penney, it was a great dinner. Thanks, Clay. Good Night, Ed."

Ed insisted on following me out to the car, which I hopped into and shut the door before he could say or do anything. He tapped on the window. "I'll call you," he said.

As I put the car in gear and started off, I yelled toward the window, "I keep pretty busy." I laughed all the way home.

Clay, Penney and I made jokes about this later. "Honestly, Lou, I'd never seen him in that dreadful toupee before. He looked like Bela Lugosi!" I told her the Ed the Plumber thought and the insurance man conversation.

Clay grinned. "I thought, incorrectly, that an insurance salesman was a notch above Alec the mailman!" The three of us laughed uproariously about the entire affair.

Later that month, Ed called. He asked if I was free to go dancing at the VFW on Saturday night. Without giving me time to answer, he chatted a bit. I finally broke in.

"Ed, thanks for the invitation, but I don't dance. And my calendar is pretty much filled up. All the time."

He signed off with "Gotcha." I wondered what that meant, and why on earth I thought I had to fib about it. But I was quite sure I wouldn't hear from him again.

I immediately made plans to go Yancey Crossing on Friday night for their little theater production of "The Mikado." It was well done, but not nearly as funny as I remembered it. I thought about how much more I might have enjoyed it if Joe Weaver had been here. Wondered if his ideas about Alec were what had driven him away. Wondered it he would have liked the Ed story.

* * *

Most of the time Buster and I remained as reclusive as we could. I grew listless with the routine of my life. With the passage of time I fell into the inertia of despair. Buster would stick very close to me on my down days.

When I would think back on things, I would think about love. Couldn't remember that I'd ever truly been in love. With Joe Weaver I had felt treasured. I decided that was good, and resigned myself to the thought that once in my life I had been a treasured woman. I had been more or less single and independent my entire life, and decided I could continue to be without much disappointment on my part.

JOE'S STORY

Joe drove the old Chevy through parts of Oklahoma, Texas, and New Mexico, almost straight through, before he stopped at the Four Corners Café to eat. When the waitress took his order, he flirted with her. She flirted back, and asked about the pickup. He left a hefty tip, made a mental note to stop by there again, and started on up to Red River. Joe was anxious to see the guys and do a little hell raising. The mountains were glorious, and driving the winding highway with little traffic was melting tension.

*　*　*

The first thing I saw when I drove into Red River was Smiley's Harley parked on the street. I parked the pickup and went into the closest bar.

As my eyes adjusted to the dark, I heard a booming "WEAVE, YOU SONOVABITCH. GET BACK HERE! Already grinning, I made my way to a big circular booth in the back corner. Smiley Milton hopped out of the booth, and slapped me on the back so hard I coughed.

"Hey, Smiley, howsit goin?" About that time, someone came up behind me and gave me a great bear hug, and lifted my feet off the ground.

"It's gotta be Michaelson! Hey Big Mike, put me down! You're crushing my lungs."

There was much arm socking, head thumping, and laughter. They ordered another pitcher of beer, and I relaxed and felt years of camaraderie flowing back. Big Mike was there; Smiley Milton; Walsh, Doc Bledsoe; and Lewis; but no Rutherford. I asked softly, "Ruthie?" It got quiet; the other guys shook their heads. Somebody said, "Here's to Rutherford." We all raised their glasses and said "To Ruthie."

"I see you're still driving that old clunker," Smiley said. And wearin' that damned ratty Aussie hat."

"Yeah, and I see you're still riding that piece of shit Harley."

"Hey, listen. At least it has some balls on it. You should see what Lewis drove up in. Go ahead, Louie, tell him what you're drivin'."

"Hey, listen guys" Lewis said mock defensively. "It's a minivan. I'm a bona fide, upstanding grandpa. You f_ _ _ with me and I'll get out the pictures of my grandkids." A chorus of hoots and raspberries and choking sounds followed this.

I turned to Walsh. "And you'd be the one driving the" I paused "limo?"

"Yessiree, Lieutenant. The limo of all vehicles, a Jeep Grand Cherokee." Much hoo haw followed this and Walsh actually blushed. "Wait'n'see" he said cryptically. "Wait'n'see."

From Lewis, "Tell 'em what you limped in on, Michaelson."

I interrupted. "Still driving the only vehicle I ever wanted, Big Mike?"

"Yep, the old lady has served me well."

"You don't mean that old bitch of a Suburban?" asked Smiley.

"Girl of my dreams" from me. "And you, Doc?"

147

"My car," said Bledsoe. "Too much car talk. Let's have a drink." He was a physician now and had previously had the ability to remain serious in any situation. He could put away a helluva lot of booze, too. But he was, as always, tight with the guys.

Walsh, Smiley, and Doc stayed to drink, and the other two took off for the condo to show me where my quarters were. I took a long hot shower, cleaned up, and sat down and raised a couple with the guys. When the other three came in, they were sloppy drunk. After much cussing and stumbling around, they all passed out on their beds. When Lewis and Big Mike decided to go find another bar and something to eat, I said, "I'll meet up with you later. Wanna look around a little."

The response was thumbs up, low wolf whistles, and winks.

I walked down to the old hotel and in the dining room ordered steak, french fries and coffee. I ate slowly, enjoying the meal and the people watching. Absent mindedly, I came very close to saving the steak bone for Buster, my favorite buddy. I moved on into the lounge, ordered a drink and did some more observing. A young cocktail waitress walked over to the table and asked if she could get me another. "I'd like another if you could sit down and have one with me."

"Oh, no, we're not allowed to drink with the customers."

"You're breaking my heart," I said.

"But I get my break in about twenty minutes. I'll be back."

I watched her cute little behind walk away. She was really a looker. Blonde, big blue eyes, and a figure that wouldn't quit. And young. Very young.

When she returned and sat down at my table, she had me order a tequila for her. *Hell,* I thought, *a tequila drinker.*

We made very little small talk before she asked if I was there alone, if I was with that biker bunch in town, if I was married, if I'd like to have a little fun.

"No; yes; no; yes," I replied. She clearly didn't understand; didn't get it at all. *Oh hell, again.*

She told her boss she was sick, got her purse, and led me out the door. "My apartment's just up here," she said. "My roommate won't be home yet."

Again, Oh double hell.

When she unlocked the door, it was apparent her roommate was, indeed, at home, with a very noisy bedroom guest. "Don't mind them, " she said. "They'll never know we're here."

I plunged ahead to the big question. "By the way, what's your name?"

"Sherry."

She led me to her bedroom, shedding clothes as she went. She shut the door. I locked the door. She started helping me get out of my clothes. By this time, I had noticed what a gorgeous body she had, and tried to forget all the "Oh hells." I was ready. I was also a little stunned by her acrobatics. Half the time I wasn't sure what she was doing, or trying to accomplish. I wrapped myself in the feel of her taut body, soft skin and the scent of flowers. I just tried to go with the flow. When

I was spent, I sat up on the side of the bed and started putting clothes on.

"You can't leave yet," she panted "I'm just getting started."

Then and there I made a decision. "Sherry, I can leave yet. I'm finished, and I'm too old for you."

As I walked down the stairs to the street, I felt terrific, laughed out loud. She never even asked me my name.

I walked in the door of the condo to find drunken bodies passed out and scattered around, snoring here and there. Sounded like a female voice from one of the bedrooms. I didn't even count to see who was there; just showered, gathered up my things and started for the door. Big Mike was sitting in the dark corner of the living room, wide awake. "So soon, Loo?"

"Oh, Mike. Yeah. Thought I'd drive by the 'Nam Memorial down at Angel Fire before I hit the trail.

"I'd like to see it, too. But I need to stay here tonight to make sure no one gets shot or maimed. Or jailed. Maybe I could head that way and meet up with you there."

"Maybe so."

"You probably won't be back next year, will you? I'm thinkin' this may be my last one."

"Dunno," I mumbled. "Next year's a long way off."

About that time Wally raised his head off the table, said "Beggus 'n cheer," and his head banged back down on the table.

I touched my hand to my forehead and flipped it toward Wally. "Beggus 'n cheer to you, bud."

Big Mike stood, smiled, and gave me a bear hug. "He said Vegas next year."

"Oh." We both laughed, big forced laughs, then simultaneously fell silent. For we knew that next year, and from now on, things wouldn't be quite the same. We were losing ground every year.

I said, "Vegas next year, old pal," and headed south down the mountain.

* * *

Maneuvering the twists and turns through the crisp mountain air, I drove with the windows rolled down. The scent of pine, the cool breeze from the windows kept him alert, but his mind was in another place.

He passed a sign that registered in his brain as Westphall Memorial about two miles after he went by it. He slowed, found a place to turn around off the highway and drove back up to the site.

It surprised me to see so many cars in the visitor parking area. This place was definitely not an advertised tourist attraction. The building was impressive, located high on a green hill, with a little path that led down to a chapel. I went inside, removed my hat, and started wandering around through the historic and colorful exhibits, the flags, the banner-size photos. The crowd was small, and everyone seemed to be speaking in near whispers. I walked back outside and took the path down to the little chapel. It was stark, but when my eyes adjusted to the light inside, my breath sucked in sharply. Mementoes, ribbons, medals, faded pictures. A letter from a soldier's mom telling how things were at home; a scribbled prayer in the front of a New Testament; a teddy bear; stacks and stacks of memories. The tears flowed spontaneously. I couldn't stop. I cried tears I'd held for years. I was crying for all the lost youth. Lives not lived. Things left undone. Why him and not me? For the moms and dads, sweethearts, and children.

When I felt limp and dry and drained of tears, I started to leave, only to notice a reverent little group waiting outside the door. I looked down, walked out, got in my pickup and started south again.

As I drove down through the mountains, my mind could scarce take in all the beauty and the winding highway along the Rio Grande. My thoughts meandered around from one thing to another. I stopped beside the road where the river was close enough to get to and tried some bits of cheese on my fishhook. Beautiful trout were jumping and flashing and making little rainbow splashes in the water. I found a bush to take a pee and spied what I believed to be bear tracks. Time to hit the road.

I thought about her. How she would have appreciated the memorial and the look at a time gone by. I thought about Lou riding along beside me, conversations about the mountains and sunsets, have . . .just stuff. Little talks and laughs about things. And of Buster riding shotgun between us.

I thought about Lou's relationship with Alec. I didn't understand what was there between the two but I made up my mind. I was determined to force a decision. On all of us.

* * *

When I reached Santa Fe, I checked into the old hotel on the downtown plaza, cleaned up, and went down to the lounge for a drink. As I sipped my beer, I noticed a signboard announcing the Santa Fe Opera. I talked to the bartender about it, got directions and just before sunset drove out to the amphitheater.

The production was "Pirates of Penzance." The place was not quite full and an attractive woman came in and sat down in front of me. She turned and asked if I was

155

alone. Even though there was other empty seats scattered throughout the arena.

"Please. Join me."

She was really good looking, and dressed in a ladies western-cut suit and really fancy looking cowboy boots. Very polished. She hopped up and moved next to me very quickly.

"Hi, I'm Yvonne." She stuck out her and gave me a soft, but firm handshake.

"Joe. Glad to meet you Yvonne.'

I just hate to sit alone at these things, don't you?"

"Don't have much opportunity," I replied."

She stared into my eyes. "You mean to sit with someone or attend these things?"

"Yes and yes."

She smiled. Her teeth shown unnaturally white in the glow of the big lights, and her eyes crinkled up at the corners.

Hot damn, I thought. A good looking woman with a sense of humor. I enjoyed the feel of her sitting beside me. The play was done well, just not as funny as I remembered it. Guess I was distracted, wondering if it would have been funnier with Lou beside me. When I hummed along with one of my favorite of the songs, Yvonne nudged me in the ribs, put her fingers to her lips and grinned "Sshhh."

After the performance I asked if she'd like to go back to my hotel and have a drink with me.

"Listen, I live just a short distance up in he hills, why don't you ride home with me for a drink, maybe a little music and dancing? I'll bring you back down to get your car later."

"Sounds terrific, Yvonne, but I don't go anywhere without my pickup." She raised her eyebrows, then grinned her crinkly grin.

I followed her winding and twisting into the hills behind Santa Fe. She drove her sleek Mercedes convertible up and parked in front of a place that looked like a log and stone ski resort. I whistled through my teeth. Whew. She's wealthy and hungry for male companionship. As I grinned to myself, I climbed down from the pickup, walked over and opened her car door. She practically jumped out of the car and into my arms, and planted a big wet kiss on me. I hadn't been kissed like that since the last time I saw Buster.

"Thank you Joe, I just love it when a man performs such polite gestures."

I didn't have to worry about being too forward. As we walked up to the stone entranceway with our arms around one another, she slid her hand down my back and squeezed my butt .

When we walked into the huge, open center room, I saw a stone fireplace covering almost an entire wall. The timbers on the high ceilings looked like an entire pine forest had been harvested.

"The bar is over there," she gestured. "Why don't you fix yourself a drink while I go slip into something more comfortable. She walked up a short staircase landing, pressed a button on the wall, and soft flames started in the big fireplace.

I glanced around at the artwork and furnishings and thought, this woman must have subscriptions to every architectural and interior decorating magazine on the market; but she's skipped some pages.

Yvonne returned to find me strolling around looking at the framed paintings on her walls. She had an eclectic collection of prints including waterfalls, mountains, pueblo art, and Santa Fe Opera posters. I was looking for velvet Elvis.

"You like?" she asked.

I turned and saw her in a filmy, see-through pink something and matching little satin thong sandals. Without those cowboy boots, I could see she had shapely calves and ankles, long beautiful legs.

"Oh yes," I said, eyeing her up and down, "I like."

"Not me, Joseph, the paintings."

"It's Joe. Just plain Joe." She ignored this.

"What are you having? I'll make us both one."

"Vodka tonic," I lied about the vodka. "But I don't care for another, thank you."

She walked over and took my glass and sat it on the bar, took my hand and said, "Good. No more preliminaries."

She reached up and kissed me, a long sensuous kiss. It almost took my breath. Then she took my arm and led me up the little landing to a huge bedroom, another fireplace, thick rugs covering the polished pine floors, and a bed that looked big enough to put up a little cabin and still have room left for a garden plot.

As she walked to the bed, dropping her negligee I could see her nude body proved just as firm as it had looked in her clothes. No sags or wrinkles. Her dark tanned skin was flawless, and it looked rosy in the glow of the firelight.

Yvonne was a passionate woman, a mature lover, and given over to moaning "Oh Joseph, Oh Joseph!" After she lay sleeping, I found the shower, apparently designed for a committee meeting, and took a long hot shower. When I returned to the bedroom, she was lying on her side with the sheet tucked primly up around her chin, smiling.

"Ready to go?" she grinned.

"Yes, I'm ready to go. Could I have a little coffee before I leave?"

"You don't mean you're leaving?" Her voice was strident, panicky.

"Yes, Yvonne. Thank you for a great night, but I have to be on my way."

She jumped out of the bed, stark naked, bent and picked up a little satin thong sandal, and threw it at me. Good aim, but I laughed when it fell limply to the floor.

"You bastard!" she screamed.

"Hey, what happened to 'Oh Joseph, Oh Joseph'?"

"I'll kill you, you two-timing son of a bitch."

When I saw her glance at the fancy shotgun mounted over the fireplace, I scrambled for the door, and yelled over my shoulder "Does this mean I don't get my coffee?"

I ran down and jumped into my pickup, and laughed out loud. I drove through the hills, back toward Santa Fe humming some little ditty I couldn't quite put a name to.

THE MOON'S STORY

On a late fall night, Buster and the woman sat on the screened in porch. The light from the big full moon shone through the trees and yard from a sky with scattered clouds. She mused, "I wonder why it's called the harvest moon?" We need to look it up, Buster. I'll bet it's something the Indians celebrated when..." Buster stood up and looked out into the night. His stub tail froze. "What is it, boy?"

About that time there was a reflection of lights out on the highway. She had a fleeting thought about locking Buster and herself in the house and calling the Sheriff. She stood and walked over to the screen door. Buster shot out the door like a bullet and headed up the drive.

In the silvery moonlight she made out the outline of a pickup with a visor. Her pulse quickened. Her knees felt weak. Then she saw the profile of an Anzac hat inside.

* * *

They sat on the porch talking as if no time had elapsed. As if there had never been a huge crack in the world. It had never occurred.

"It gets pretty stuffy tryin' to sleep in that bunkroom. I see you redecorated and got the new furniture and stuff. It's a great place.

His words came tumbling out. Hurried. Almost stammering.

She bristled. "Now you listen to me."

"Hear me out please."

She waited.

"I found that old spring cot in one of the stalls and fixed it up, and thought I might see if you would let me sleep on the west porch, to catch the evening breeze."

She grinned inside. *This is going to be a cool story.* "I thought you'd fixed that fan out there last summer?"

"I did, Lou. But that's still just moving air around. It's not like getting the crisp night air of autumn. Buster could guard me."

The woman giggled. "Oh all right. I know when you and Buster make up your minds there's no use trying to argue."

"I know, I know. I remember the rules. Don't try anything. I won't" He smiled a crooked little smile she hadn't seen before.

She went in and got ready for bed. She could hear the sound of him moving the cot in, scraping it across the floor, talking softly to Buster.

That was stupid, Lou. He'll be right outside your window. You'll have to keep the lights off in the bedroom. Hope I don't snore. Hope he doesn't snore. I know Buster snores.

Then all was quiet.

EPILOGUE

A short time later she heard his voice drift through her window:

"A bunch of boys were whooping it up in the Malamute saloon;

The kid that handles the music-box was hitting a jag-time tune;

Back of the bar, in a solo game sat Dangerous Dan McGrew,

And watching his luck was his light-o'-love, the lady that's known as Lou."

Joe Weaver's voice rose and fell rhythmically. He was reciting with great feeling. Lou felt chills up and down her spine.

"When out of the night, which was fifty below, and into the din and the glare,

There stumbled a miner fresh from the creeks, dog-dirty, and loaded for bear.

166

He looked like a man with a foot in the grave and scarcely the strength of a louse,

Yet he tilted a poke of dust on the bar, and he called for drinks for the house."

Lou felt her heart speeding up. She knew this poem well, one of her favorites. She cleared her throat softly. He kept up the narrative:

"And I got to figgering who he was, and wondered what he'd do, And I turned my head—and there watching him was the lady that's known as Lou"

"Were you ever out in the Great Alone, when the moon was awful clear,

And the icy mountains hemmed you in with a silence you most could hear."

She sat up on the side of the bed and took a deep breath.

"Then I ducked my head, and the lights went out, and two guns blazed in the dark,

167

And a woman screamed, and the lights went up and two men lay stiff and stark.

Pitched on his head, and pumped full of lead, was Dangerous Dan McGrew,

While the man from the creeks lay clutched to the breast of the lady that's known as Lou."

She rose from her bed, tiptoed barefoot out to the screened in porch, sat down on the side of his cot. Joe Weaver kept reciting. She lay down and snuggled her backside against him. The harvest moon, shining through the branches of the maple, made silvery shadows. He gave the back of her neck a soft kiss, wrapped his arms around her and kept reciting . . .

The little Brittany lay dreaming the sounds of the night.

III.

SQUIRT'S KITE

Hi, I'm Robert Benjamin Markham. My dad is Robert Benjamin Markham, too. I found out it's pretty cool to be called Benjamin instead of Junior. Don't like Junior.

Our wood frame house is back about a hundred feet from the main street, and big oaks and maples shade the yard and screened-in porch across the front of the house. Sometimes, when Dad's in a good mood he'll let my little brother and me sleep out on the porch. We have a big old red barn next to the house that dad uses for a workshop. And there's a giant apple tree next to the side of the house that faces the barn.

Dad drives in to D.C. every morning to work as an architect. He's always bragging to Mom's family about "We enjoy small-town life at the doorstep to the nation's capitol." I think it's neat. He's shown me some of the stores he's designed. The relatives just look at him, ya know? Like if he's never driven a tractor there must be something wrong there.

That summer I spent most of my time daydreaming about all the things I'd do next summer. My buddy Justin had a job at the box factory, and my best friend Zack was spending the summer with his dad in Texas. That left me at home with a bicycle, a kid brother, and scrounging up odd jobs. I got a job mowing Mrs. Patterson's yard once a week, but it didn't pay enough to add up very fast. In June she offered me an extra ten bucks to clean out her garage.

I started early on a Saturday morning. It was hot and dusty in the garage, and the only light was from the door in front. The first thing I started on was moving stacks of musty, old newspapers out front so I could get to the other magazines, boxes and junk piled up in the back. Those crumbly old piles of newspapers were heavy, and I had to divide the stacks to be able to move them. I finally worked out this trick of kick-scooting the stacks out to the driveway. A little after 10:00 in the morning Mrs. Patterson came out of the house with a glass of ice water and told me to take a break. We tried to make conversation. If you've ever tried to talk to the top of a head of silver-blue hairs held together by a lot of pink scalp, you get the picture.

She talked about her begonias and the late Mr. Patterson. While I was trying to figure out what he was late for, she switched the conversation to "your father, Robert Senior. He was a fine boy. When he was about your age he helped the late Mr. Patterson scrape and paint this very garage."

She got misty-eyed and gazed at the garage for a while. Finally, we gave up on conversation, and she went back inside.

I sat down in the back where it was dark and cooler. I was thinking about how to talk my Mom into teaching me to drive her car. Out of the corner of my eye I saw an old yellowed newspaper with a giant headline: "GLENN A-OK! FRIENDSHIP 7 LANDS."

I eased the paper out of the pile. It was dated February 12, 1962. That was before I was born! The guy in the picture was grinning like crazy and holding his thumb up. The whole idea was kind of funny. All they did was shoot him up there and he went around the earth a couple of times and then splashed down in the ocean, for cripes sake. Still, I liked the idea of the first astronaut; you know, like a pioneer? I folded the newspaper and went and stuck it in the basket of my bike.

I got all the papers and magazines moved and stacked out front. I gathered up the trash in boxes, and swept and locked up. I knocked, and Mrs. Patterson came to the door. She already had a check made out to Robert Junior in her fine, scrawly handwriting. Everybody called me by my middle name. But I decided not to point that out to her right now. She thanked me. . I thanked her. She started in on how glad she was to have that done, and before she could steer things back around to begonias and Mr. Patterson, I hopped on my bike, yelled, "Thanks again," and took off.

When I rode into our yard, I saw my kid brother Timmy in Dad's workshop in the barn with a bunch of hacked up grocery bags spread all over the floor around him. He had his head bent over the workbench when I walked up behind him.

"Whatcha doin, Squirt?"

"I'm 'onna build me a kite."

"Dad say you could use that spruce?"

"Huh?"

"Squirt, you'd better leave Dad's lumber alone. He'll be mad as hell if you cut on that spruce."

"Mom said don't cuss, Benjy."

"Listen, Squirt, you holler in and tell Mom you're going to ride to town with me and we'll go . . ."

"But Benj! I gotta build me a kite. Eric Fisher's mom bought him a great big green dinosaur kite, biggern this barn and ... and Benj, he don't even know how to fly a kite. And if I get one built and show him how I can fly a kite, he might let me hold the string on his dinosaur. We're goin' out to the bluff tomorrow right after Sunday dinner, and I gotta have my kite ready by then."

"Get your shoes, Squirt, and I'll take you to Jensen's. We'll get you some balsa and build you a real kite. Go use the bathroom first."

You gotta do that with little brothers. Seven-year olds can be a real pain in the you-know-what sometimes, but Squirt was okay most of the time. I mean he never messed around with my stuff. Boy, he was real smart, too. Besides that, I was his hero. Finally, he hopped on the back of my bike and I peddled down to Jensen's Mercantile. Jensen's was the best store in Bird Creek. You could get anything there. That's where Dad got his paint, Mom got needles and thread, and sometimes Mr. Jensen had little bitty turtles in a bowl on the counter. I knew we could get some balsa wood there.

We hopped off my bike, went in, and walked straight to the back where the balsa sticks were.

"Whaddya think, Squirt? Does this seem pretty straight to you?" I held one stick up and sighted down it to see if it was warped. Then I handed it to The Squirt. He took it like I did and held it up to his nose and sniffed the end of it! I guess he thought I had smelled it. Mr. Jensen watched all this and started to laugh except he saw I wasn't going to.

"Well, what's the verdict, Timothy? Think that's satisfactory?"

"Yessir, Mr. Jensen. Me 'n Benjy's gonna build a kite, and I get to fly it!"

"Well, Timothy, you got any string? Don't you and Benjamin need to pick out some twine, too?"

Just then I started liking Mr. Jensen a whole lot better. Squirt looked up at me like I was gonna yell at him or somethin'.

"Sure, Squirt. Better get two spools. If you're gonna fly a kite right, your gonna want enough string to fly it till it's a mere speck on the horizon."

Squirt giggled in that real squeaky way little kids have and picked up two spools of twine.

You ever seen one of those pictures of Jesus where they have this bright circle of light around his head? Well, that's another thing about The Squirt. His face gave off light like that sometimes, and he was just this scrawny little kid with a cowlick and a crooked tooth in front. His face was lit up like that now. It *almost* made me forget about spending my money on him.

Squirt yakked all the way home. I tuned him out and was thinking about how I could earn some more cash. Maybe see about sweeping the barbershop in the evenings. I was still thinking when The Squirt poked me.

"Won't we, Benj?"

"Won't what, Squirt?"

"We'll make it go so high it'll go clear past the clouds, and Eric Fisher's dinosaur won't never find it!"

When we got into the yard, Mom stuck her head out the door on the screened-in porch. "Benjamin, you and Timothy hurry and wash up. Dinner's on the table."

Squirt was in such a hurry to get back out to the barn, Dad had to raise his voice at him to finish his dinner. Ordinarily when someone yells at him, Squirt gets real quiet; but nothing could dampen his excitement over that kite. He was so fidgety he was makin' me nervous, but his green beans finally disappeared about the time Dad scooted his chair back from the table.

"Now, Benjy?"

"Sure, Squirt. Come on." Mom had to remind us about clearing the table, and Dad asked if we needed any help in the barn.

"Thanks, Dad, but I'm buildin' a kite and Benjy's helpin'."

"Okay, boys. Just be careful, and put the tools back where you find them."

We made a space on the workbench, and I showed Squirt how to draw the outline of the kite on paper, and how to figure the length of the sticks. We used the newspaper I'd picked up from Mrs. Patterson's. It really looked neat to have this huge kite with a real live astronaut waving from the front of it. Squirt got a real bang out of that. At last we got the sticks and the picture balanced just right. I started showing him how to notch the ends of the sticks.

"Oh, Benjy, p-l-e-a-s-e let me." I knew both Dad and Mom would have kittens if the Squirt got cut, but I let him have my pocket-knife anyway. Mom came close to fits when I just showed him how to climb the apple tree and peek in the kitchen window.

Squirt notched the second stick very carefully. Ya see what I'm talkin about? The

Squirt's smart and he pays attention. He stuck his tongue out the corner of his mouth like I've seen Dad do, and worked real careful. Did a perfect job, too. Still, I was awful glad when he handed my knife back to me.

Mom yelled at him to come in to bed. He tried "P-l-e-a-s-e," but it didn't work with her. Then he got these two real big pitiful tears that went plop plop right on the floor of the barn.

" Listen, Squirt. You go on and go to bed. In the morning after church this glue will be dry. When we get home, we'll rig the bridle. Then all you need to do is take it out and fly it. Eric Fisher will still be trying to get his dinosaur off the ground."

Squirt ran over and threw his arms around my knees and squeezed. His arms felt real skinny and frail, but it still nearly knocked me over.

"Oh, Benjy, you'll go with me, won't you? You'll help me? You'll show me...Please?" His eyes were still wet and his lashes were shiny from where those tears had squeezed out.

Night, Squirt." I went over to do the gluing part. I guess there must have been some really strong solvent in that glue or something because my eyes started burning. He could be a real nuisance sometimes, that little Squirt.

Mom came out later and watched a while. "Where'd you get that newspaper?"

I explained to her and told her about Eric Fisher's dinosaur and Squirt wanting his own kite.

"I know, Benjamin. Your brother was so excited. I'm sure it'll be a while before he goes to sleep. He begged me to let the two of you sleep on the screened in porch." She paused. "Quite a celebrity. He became a U.S. Senator."

"Who?"

"The astronaut in the picture. Timothy idolizes you, you know."

"Mom, the Squirt idolizes anybody over four feet tall."

"I brought some scraps for the tail." She held up pieces of bright shiny cloth.

"This red satin was left over from when you were a lightening bug in second grade."

She was staring at what I was doing, but it was like she was seeing something else.

"The yellow and blue is from the scarecrow costume I made you when you were nine. I thought Timmy would like bright colors for the tail."

"Gee, thanks, Mom. Those are neat colors." She reached up and flicked the bangs out of my eyes. I haven't worn bangs since I was Squirt's age. I don't know how long she's had to stretch to reach my imaginary bangs. I never noticed it before.

"Son, your father and I are very proud of the example you set for your little brother." She turned and went back into the house. Grownups, huh.

The Sunday skies were sunny and bright blue with cotton ball clouds, and we made it all the way through church with Dad only having to thump Squirt on the back of the head once. On the way home he had to threaten him again. The only time the Squirt's mouth closed was when we all went out to the barn and he saw the kite that I had finished, with the red, blue and yellow streamers on the tail. His eyes got big as saucers, and he shrieked "Oh Benjy! Is it mine?" He ran over and walked all around it, fingering the tail, looking at it some more, skipping around it and clapping his hands. Dad was right behind him except he managed not to skip and clap.

"Benjamin, you did a really fine job."

"Oh, Squirt, too, Dad. He marked the paper and notch . . .he helped a lot."

We carefully loaded the kite, its tail and string into the trunk of the car and drove out to the bluff. Eric Fisher and his dad weren't there, but Squirt and I got out and launched the kite.

The kite took off on the first little puff of breeze, and rose swiftly in the steady air. Pretty soon Squirt's astronaut rode right on top of the wind.

That current was so strong I was afraid the line would cut Squirt's hand. But when I offered to help, he gave me this big grin, and from between clenched teeth said, "so kay, Benj, I got her!"

Dad and I both wanted to take the string, to help him, to hold it. Really, we both wanted to get the feel of it, to keep him from hurting his hand, but one look at his face and we stayed quiet.

"We did it! Benjy, we did it!" Squirt was running around like crazy. We had tied both spools of twine together and let out all the string.

Mom, looking up at the sky, with her hand shading her eyes, shouted, "Oh, Timmy! It's wonderful!"

Dad yelled, "Go, Son. Go!"

Then the line snapped.

The kite sailed off into the distance and was getting smaller and smaller. Squirt's face got that light around it like I told you about. Most little kids would have cried to lose their kite. Not The Squirt.

"Know what, Benjy?" He was panting and rubbing his hand. "Can't no dinosaurs fly like that. Just astronauts. Oh Look, Benjy, look! It's a near speck on the horizon!"

It was a shining moment. Yeah, Squirt's kite was somethin' special.

EPILOGUE

Washington, D.C. (UPA)

AN FBI SWAT team was dispatched to the home of Sen. David McGlamery Sunday when a missile landed in the senator's backyard. Thirty guests had gathered for a garden party which was disrupted when the projectile landed in their midst. No injuries were reported. Federal Agents are conducting an investigation to determine if there is extremist involvement. The projectile resembled a crude kite constructed of newspaper which featured a photo of astronaut John Glenn, waving triumphantly from the space capsule, Friendship 7. Former U.S. Senator John Glenn's historic space flight was documented in the 1962 newspaper article. Senator Glenn's spokesperson denied any knowledge. Agents are trying to determine if this indicates a threat against Glenn. The White House had no comment. Inside sources say the kite has been sent to the FBI lab for further analysis.

ABOUT THE AUTHOR

The author is retired from a long career in business. She and her husband Roger live in Northeast Texas where she is working on a new volume of short stories and poems. Ms. Redick is a member of Silver Leos Writers Guild at Texas A&M-Commerce.

Majel has chosen to publish a large print edition to accommodate low vision readers like her.

CPSIA information can be obtained
at www.ICGtesting.com
Printed in the USA
BVHW040205140920
588764BV00012B/299

9 781461 040255